GUNS BLAZING IN THE NIGHT . . .

This time Slocum didn't let the opportunity pass. As the muzzles flashed, he aimed at the center figure, fired quickly three times, then hit the deck.

His second shot had found its target, and the third had also hit someone, probably the same man. . . .

DON'T MISS THESE
ALL-ACTION WESTERN SERIES
FROM THE BERKLEY PUBLISHING GROUP

THE GUNSMITH by J. R. Roberts
>Clint Adams was a legend among lawmen, outlaws, and ladies. They called him . . . the Gunsmith.

LONGARM by Tabor Evans
>The popular long-running series about U.S. Deputy Marshal Long—his life, his loves, his fight for justice.

LONE STAR by Wesley Ellis
>The blazing adventures of Jessica Starbuck and the martial arts master, Ki. Over eight million copies in print.

SLOCUM by Jake Logan
>Today's longest-running action western. John Slocum rides a deadly trail of hot blood and cold steel.

JAKE LOGAN

AMBUSH AT
APACHE ROCKS

BERKLEY BOOKS, NEW YORK

AMBUSH AT APACHE ROCKS

A Berkley Book / published by arrangement with
the author

PRINTING HISTORY
Berkley edition/November 1993

ISBN: 0-425-13981-6

BERKLEY®
Berkley Books are published by
The Berkley Publishing Group, 200 Madison Avenue,
New York, New York 10016.
BERKLEY and the "B" design are trademarks of
Berkley Publishing Corporation.

PRINTED IN THE UNITED STATES OF AMERICA

10 9 8 7 6 5 4 3 2 1

AMBUSH AT
APACHE ROCKS

1

The sign said "Rattigan's Saloon." The paint was peeling, but the letters were still reasonably visible, and John Slocum was not one to care much about appearances. When he was as thirsty as he was at the moment, he didn't care at all. As long as Rattigan, or whoever was standing behind the bar, was willing to pour, Slocum was willing to drink. Las Cruces wasn't much to look at. It had the feel of a place hanging on by its collective fingernails, hoping a stiff breeze didn't come along and blow it away altogether. He didn't expect that Rattigan's would be busy.

When he pushed aside the butterfly doors and stepped inside, he immediately wrinkled his nose to lessen the assault of damp sawdust and beer. The rank tang of fermentation was a smell as old as Noah, maybe even older. Slocum shook his head, and wondered how it could be men had such an attachment to the wretched stuff.

A few hands were sitting at a table. They were

1

not talking much, and punctuating what little conversation there was with the loud slap of playing cards on damp wood. They glanced his way
for a moment, one of them arrested his hand in
mid deal, nodded, then continued to pass out the
cards.

Walking to the bar, Slocum tilted his hat back
and nodded to a beefy man with rolled sleeves
mopping at the bar with a damp rag in each hand.
The man was not fat, just big, and his barrel chest
strained at a denim shirt as his thick arms worked
their circles on the scarred wood.

"Howdy," he said. "What'll you have?"

Fishing for a handful of coins in his pocket,
Slocum said, "Beer, please."

The barman's face broke into a grin. "Please, huh?
Now there's a word that don't get much use around
these parts. First one'll be on the house—kind of a
nod toward civility." Cocking his head toward the
table full of cardplayers, he added, "Maybe you can
give those fellas a little lesson in manners, while
you're at it."

Tucking the rags under the ties of his apron,
he drew a beer, scraped the head down with a
wooden stick, and set it down in front of Slocum.
Then, sticking one giant hand across the bar, he
said, "Name's Phil Rattigan."

Slocum nodded, took the great paw in his own,
and shook it. "John Slocum," he said.

"You look a might dusty, Mister Slocum,"
Rattigan observed. "Come a far piece, did you?"

"El Paso," Slocum said, lifting the beer mug and
taking a long pull. "Four days on the trail."

"Reckon you'll want another beer," Rattigan said,

smiling, "The next one ain't free, though."

Slocum laughed. "Too thirsty to give a damn," he said.

Rattigan didn't wait for the mug to be empty. He grabbed a second one, drew the beer, then slid it down the bar. "There you go, Mister Slocum. Just grab a breath between glasses. I don't want nobody to drown his first day in town."

"I can swim, Mister Rattigan," Slocum said. "And I'm thirsty enough so it won't matter much. Reckon I could drink a lake dry, if I was to fall in."

Rattigan snatched a shot glass from a shelf under a long mirror behind the bar, wiped it clean with the tail of his apron, and poured himself a shot. "Bushmill's," he said, "about the best there is, you ask me." He tossed the shot off in a single swallow, then rubbed his lips with the back of one thick wrist. "Irish," he said, "like me. Ever tried it?"

Slocum shook his head. "Can't say as I have. I'm pretty much a bourbon drinker when I want something with a little kick to it."

"Kick?" Rattigan asked. "You want something that'll make a mule sit up and take notice, toss this down." He grabbed another shot glass and poured a double, then pushed it toward Slocum with his fingertips. "Go on, try it. On the house, in case you're wondering."

Rattigan folded his arms and leaned back against the shelf with his eyes fixed on Slocum's face. Setting down the beer, Slocum picked up the shot glass, took a sniff, and nodded approvingly. Then, with a nod, he tossed it down.

"Good," he said with his voice not working quite right. "Strong, too."

"Strong ain't the word for it. I know miners use it to blast with," Rattigan said.

"Why don't you shut up about that damn stuff?" somebody asked.

Rattigan glared past Slocum, who turned to see who had spoken.

One of the men at the card table was glaring back. "Phil, you go on and on about that damn stuff like it was God's gift."

"I can't expect some ignorant cowpoke to appreciate the finer things in life," Rattigan said. "But I figure Mister Slocum here, might have a little breeding."

"Don't look so special to me," the cowhand said. "Look's like any other trail bum I ever seen."

"Ray, maybe you just better pay attention to your cards. Never known you to handle two things at once before. No sense pushing yourself too hard on a day off, is there?"

The rest of the cardplayers laughed, but Ray wasn't amused. He got to his feet and started toward the bar. One of the men at the table reached out and grabbed him by the arm, but Ray shook loose, and continued toward Rattigan. "You ain't half as funny as you think you are, Phil," he said. When he reached the bar, he leaned on it, and looked at Slocum. "What do you think, cowboy, is he funny?"

"Made me laugh," Slocum said.

"You think he's so funny, maybe you want to step outside and tell me why. How about it? I don't get it. Maybe you can explain it to me."

"Let it be, Ray," Rattigan said. "Go on back and finish your card game."

Ray shook his head slowly. "There you go again, Phil. Always tellin' me what to do and what not to do."

Rattigan smiled. "You know, Ray, I figure it's about time *somebody* explained a few things to you. Unfortunately, your father must have neglected his responsibilities somewhere along the line, because I can't believe you'd have such bad manners if he'd done his job."

Ray leaned forward, and reached across the bar. At the same moment he went for his gun, but Slocum saw the move and grabbed his arm by the wrist just as the pistol cleared the holster.

Twisting Ray's arm, Slocum yanked the gun free, stuck it in his own gun belt, and stepped away. Turning to watch the men at the table, Slocum said. "Anybody want to take this man home before he gets somebody hurt?"

Ray jerked his arm loose, and backed away a step or two. "Phil," he said, "seems like you let anybody drink in here these days."

"Not anymore, Ray," Rattigan answered. "So I'd be much obliged if you'd take your business elsewhere for a few weeks. Maybe once you have a chance to think things over, you'll straighten out. I sure hope so, because if you don't, somebody's gonna get hurt bad."

"The hell with you, Rattigan. It ain't like you got the only bar in town."

"Maybe not, but as far as I know, I got the only one that still serves you—until today, that is." Leaning around to peer past the glowering Ray, Rattigan hollered, "Bobby, one of you boys want to take Mister Sadler on home?"

"He can find his own way home, Phil," one of the hands answered. The others laughed, but Rattigan got angry.

"I'm not jokin', Bobby. I don't want him in here. The sooner you get him home, the more likely he is to live till next payday."

A tall, gangly cowboy stood up, looked once at his cards, then folded them, and tossed them onto the table. "Aw, hell, I ain't holding nothing anyhow. Might as well do it myself."

The tall cowhand walked to the bar and reached out to grab hold of Sadler's arm. "Come on, Ray. Let's get some fresh air."

Sadler jerked his arm loose, and in the same movement launched himself at Slocum. He swung from the heels, but Slocum saw it coming, ducked out of the way, and landed a sharp hook to his ribs as Sadler stumbled by. The drunken cowboy grunted as the air was crushed from his lungs, and doubled over as he fell to the floor.

The one Rattigan called Bobby glared at Slocum, but said nothing to him. Instead, he reached down to pat Sadler on the shoulder. "Come on, Ray. Seems like we ain't welcome here right now."

Slocum heard the scrape of chairs and saw the three other men pushing away from the table, and he tensed. But they didn't make any moves that might indicate they had gunplay on their minds.

"Don't let him puke on the floor, Bobby," Rattigan said. He leaned over the bar and glanced at Sadler, who was still gasping for breath and groaning as if he was about to vomit.

Reaching up for the edge of the bar, Sadler hauled himself to his feet. He looked hard at Slocum, then at his pistol, which was still stuck in Slocum's belt. "Gimme my gun," he said.

Slocum nodded. He pulled the pistol from his belt, looked at it a moment, broke it open, and dumped the shells onto the bar. Then, closing the pistol again, he tossed it to Sadler, who tried to snatch it out of the air, but missed and sent it clattering across the floor.

Bobby went over, picked it up, and walked back. Jamming it into Sadler's holster, he looked at Slocum. "No need to make a fool out of the man," he said.

"He didn't need my help for that," Slocum answered.

"You better not hang around too long," Bobby said. "If you're passin' through, you better keep on goin'. If you ain't, maybe you better think about movin' on."

He took Sadler by the shoulder and started to tug him toward the door. The other three hands shuffled past, all of them staring at Slocum as they moved toward the door. They pushed on out into the sunlight, and Bobby dragged Sadler the rest of the way outside, but the drunken cowhand broke free and pushed back inside.

"You best think about what Bobby said, Mister," he warned. "I'll see you again, and I'll be sober."

Slocum nodded. "That's a start," he said.

Sadler turned away, letting the doors swing shut. Slocum took a deep breath.

"Sorry about that," Rattigan said. "He's a mean one even when he ain't drinkin', but sometimes he gets a snootful and we get to see the real Ray Sadler."

"Not a pretty sight," Slocum said.

"You know, I don't mean to be tellin' you your business, but I'd think about what Bobby said. Sadler might take a run at you, as likely as not when you ain't looking. That's the kind of man he is."

"Well," Slocum said. "I wasn't planning on staying, anyhow."

"That'd be best, I think. It ain't like you was to run from trouble, after all—if you was just passing through, I mean."

"I've had my share of trouble, Phil," Slocum said, laughing, "and I've seen worse than Sadler, for sure. But I learned one thing, anyhow, and that's that there's enough trouble in the world without a man having to look for it."

"One more on the house," Rattigan offered.

"That'd be much appreciated."

"You figuring on staying the night, or you moving on this afternoon?"

Slocum shrugged. "It's all the same to me—why?"

"I got rooms to rent, you need one?"

"We'll see."

2

Slocum was glad he'd decided to take the room. He hadn't realized just how exhausted he was until he lay down on the bed and closed his eyes. It was well on toward sundown by the time they opened again. He was hungry, so he got up and pulled his boots back on before walking to the lace-curtained window and looking out into the street. Las Cruces wasn't big, and the traffic in the streets, what little there was, was quiet. He watched a wagon, its wheels creaking plaintively, roll down the center of the street, and pull up in front of the general store.

A big man with a handlebar mustache, his ample girth restrained only slightly by a dark blue, pinstriped canvas apron, stood in the doorway of the store. He watched as the driver of the wagon set the brake, looped the reins around the brake handle, and climbed down.

The big man said something Slocum couldn't hear. Whatever the wagon driver said in response made the storekeeper laugh, and he patted his stomach before turning to go inside. The man with the wagon stepped onto the boardwalk, turned to look up the street, then glanced at the sun before following the merchant inside.

Slocum let the lace curtain drop, walked to a ladder-back chair that was the room's only furniture besides the bed, and grabbed his gun belt. He buckled it on and walked to the door. Glancing around the room as if he'd forgotten something, although for the life of him he couldn't imagine what, he opened the door and stepped out into the hall.

He closed and locked the door, then tucked the key into his pocket. The hall was carpeted, but the carpet had seen better days, like much of the rest of Las Cruces. At the head of the stairs he stopped for a moment, listening. Something had caught his ear, but he wasn't sure what.

Descending the stairs, he saw Rattigan behind the bar. The Irishman glanced over, waved at him, and said, "I reckon you're hungry, Slocum."

Slocum nodded. "Sure am."

"Try the Silver Skillet. Food's good, there's lots of it, and the price is fair. Besides, I'm kind of sweet on Maggie Carson, the gal who runs it. Any time I can throw a little business her way, I try."

Slocum laughed. "Looks to me like you might take a few meals there yourself."

Rattigan looked at his stomach. "You noticed, huh?" He laughed. "I can't get enough of Maggie *or* her cooking. I'll be down myself in a few minutes, soon as my relief man gets here. You want to wait, I'll walk over with you, introduce you. Might even cadge us dessert on the house. Maggie makes some mighty fine pie." He winked, patted his gut again, and added, "Most of this here is pie, matter of fact. If I could lay off it, I'd be a whole lot skinnier."

The bartender drew a beer, passed it across the bar, and said, "Here, this'll take the edge off until we get to the Skillet."

Slocum thanked him, took a pull on the beer, and sat on one of the half dozen bar stools. "Tell me about Ray Sadler," he said.

"Ain't much to tell, really. What do you want to know?"

Slocum shrugged. "I don't know. Seems like he's a stick of dynamite with the fuse lit. Seen his kind before, but I've never been able to figure it out."

Rattigan tilted his head to one side, as if he were listening for something, then took a deep breath. Letting it out in a sigh, he said, "Works for Tom Childress, over at the Broken C. Childress's been here almost as long as I have—'bout ten years or so, I guess. Has a big spread out west of town. Cattle mostly, some horses. Does a good business with the army. He has their beef contract, has almost every year since he got here. Some folks say it's connections, others say he's just a good businessman. Me, I wouldn't know. Got no connections and don't know much about business."

"I can tell, all the free drinks you give away."

Rattigan laughed. "Oh, hell, that was just my appreciation. Nice to see somebody put Ray Sadler on his butt for a change. It's usually the other way around. He's been working for Childress six, seven years, I guess. Been ornery as a skunk since the day he got here. I figure he'll go out the same way, less somebody puts him in a pine box."

"What's he do for Childress?"

Rattigan shrugged. "Cowhand—foreman the last two years. Tom must have twenty-five, thirty thousand head. Lot of work keepin' that many cows in line. Ray's good at what he does, I guess, or Childress wouldn't keep him around. Can't afford to have a foreman who ain't no good. He likes his drink, though, and, like I told you, he's got a nasty temper."

"Seems like a bit of a bully," Slocum suggested.

"More than a bit, you ask me. I've had to brain him more than once in here. He gets a little whiskey under his belt, then starts lookin' for a fight. Mostly, he picks on smaller men, as you would expect. I was kind of surprised to see him light into you like he done. And he seems to have a particular dislike for small ranchers. Don't know why for sure, although I have my suspicions, but almost every time I had to break up a fight, it was Ray goin' head-to-head with one or another of the homesteaders around here. As like as night, gangin' up with a few of the Broken C boys—that's his way. He likes the odds in his favor."

"Childress puts up with it?"

Rattigan laughed outright. "Oh, hell yes. If Tom had his way, he'd own everything from here to Arizona. He's made an offer to just about everybody around here at one time or another. And he don't like it when somebody says no—which most do—at least at first."

"What do you mean?" Slocum asked. "At first? Then what? They change their minds?"

"More often than not. Some folks think maybe that's Ray's part-time job: persuading folks to sell to Childress." He shrugged. "Just talk, as far as I know, but you can't never tell."

"Sounds like a match made in heaven," Slocum said.

"Oh, they deserve each other, that's for certain. Tom's about as prickly a fella as you could want to meet. Little banty fella, but he's got a temper fit for a man my size. He'll call you out if you just look at him cross-eyed."

The doors were pushed open, and Slocum found himself looking at the thinnest human being he'd ever seen.

"Twigs," Rattigan said. "It's about time you got here. I'm about to starve to death, and so is Mister Slocum."

The man called Twigs smiled. "Missin' a meal or two won't hurt you none, Phil," he said. "Fact is, I could use a few extra pounds my own self. Maybe I ought to run down to the Skillet before I start work."

Rattigan cursed under his breath, but was shaking his head and laughing at the same time. "Damn you, Twigs, sometimes I think maybe you got a mean streak."

Then, turning to Slocum, he said, "That there collection of tinder is Randall Hardaway, but, for reasons that a blind man can plainly see, we call him Twigs."

Slocum stuck out a hand. "John Slocum," he said as Twigs took his hand and shook it.

"Pleased to meet you, Mister Slocum."

"We're gonna go on down to the Skillet for dinner. Be back in about an hour."

Twigs took a look around the saloon. The handful of patrons weren't likely to tax even so spindly a bartender, and Twigs nodded. "Looks like the evening rush ain't started yet, Phil."

Rattigan nodded. "Not yet, but you know how it is. Just give a holler if you need me sooner."

Twigs moved behind the bar as Rattigan took off the damp apron he was wearing, rolled it into a ball, and tossed it at Hardaway, who ducked as it sailed past, then snaked out an arm and caught it by the strings.

"See you fellers later," he said.

Rattigan rolled his sleeves down and smoothed his thinning straw-colored hair with an anxious hand.

Twigs noticed. "Take more than that to make Maggie notice you, Phil," he said.

Rattigan glared as he pushed out into the dying sunlight.

"Just up the street, Mister Slocum," he said. "I hope you're hungry, because you are about to have one of the best meals since the last time you ate your grandma's cookin'."

Slocum glanced at the general store, where the wagon was still sitting with its bed now half full of supplies. As he walked past, he spotted the driver staggering toward the door of the store with a heavy sack of flour in his arms. The man felt for the boardwalk, stepped down, then moved to the wagon, where he leaned over, and dropped the heavy sack with a dull thud. A cloud of flour ballooned into the sunlight, and seemed to catch fire for a moment, then disappeared.

"Howdy, Jason," Rattigan said.

"Phil," the man answered, nodding. "How you doing?"

Rattigan waved a hand as if to say "I've been better and I've been worse." At the front of the Silver Skillet, Rattigan pawed at his hair once more, then opened the door, and nodded for Slocum to precede him inside.

A table by the window was empty, and Rattigan headed straight for it. "This here's my table," he said, sitting down and motioning for Slocum to do the same. Take all my meals here. Breakfast, dinner, and supper."

"That you do, Phil Rattigan, but the table's mine, all the same."

Slocum turned to see who had spoken, but he knew by the sudden smile on Rattigan's face that it had to be Maggie Carson. And as soon as his eyes registered her face, he knew why Rattigan was acting like a schoolboy. Maggie Carson was stunning.

"See, didn't I tell you she was something to look at?" Rattigan blurted, getting out of his chair.

Maggie blushed, glared at Rattigan, and said, "Just you hush, Philip Rattigan. Mind your manners." Then, turning to Slocum, she smiled. "Margaret Carson," she said. "Don't you pay any attention to Mister Rattigan."

Slocum got awkwardly to his feet. "He's right, though, Miss Carson. You are a beautiful woman."

Looking at Slocum but inquiring of Rattigan, she said, "Aren't you going to tell me the gentleman's name, Phil? I think I can tell him where he might get his eyes checked, and maybe a good pair of spectacles while he's at it."

"John Slocum," Slocum said.

Maggie smiled broadly. "It's a pleasure to meet you, Mister Slocum," she said, extending her right hand. Slocum clasped it in his own, and was surprised at the strength of her grip.

"I was just—what was that?"

"Sounded like a gunshot to me," Rattigan offered.

Slocum let go of Maggie's hand, and cocked his ear toward the door.

Another sharp crack sounded somewhere in the street, and all the diners stopped with their forks frozen in midair, and their knives arrested only halfway through a piece of steak or a pork chop.

Slocum moved toward the door. "Where you going, Slocum?" Rattigan called, but Slocum was already halfway to the door. He reached it in two quick strides and turned the knob as Rattigan got to his feet.

As he swung the door open, a third shot, this one sounding very loud without the door to dampen the sound, shattered glass somewhere down the block.

"Wait for me!" Rattigan hollered, moving around the table. "Wait for me!"

"You men be careful," Maggie said. "You hear me, Phil?"

3

Slocum rushed into the street as a fourth shot exploded. He heard the bullet whistle past him and slam into a wooden column supporting the porch roof of the Silver Skillet. Instinctively, he dove headlong, even though he knew the shot could not have been aimed at him. Up the block, he saw several men on horseback with their pistols drawn. They were jerking the reins of their mounts, and starting toward the far end of town.

One of the men spotted Slocum, shouted something, and aimed his pistol. Slocum tried to reach for the Colt Navy on his hip, but his arm was pinned under his body. As he rolled onto his side to get his arm free, a bullet gouged the dirt just inches from his face. It sent a shower of sand at him that stung his face and momentarily blinded him. He kept rolling as three more shots slammed into the earth around him.

Blinking to rid his eyes of the sand grains, he shook his head, but the sharp edges of the sand scraped under his lids, and he was forced to keep

17

his eyes shut tight. He heard Rattigan yelling, then felt someone grab him by the arms and drag him across the hard-packed dirt of the street. Two more shots rang out, and once more he heard the whistle of a bullet, but this time he heard the splat of one striking flesh, and then a groan. The pressure on his arms slackened momentarily, and he knew Rattigan had been hit.

"Phil, you all right?"

Groaning through clenched teeth, Rattigan mumbled something Slocum didn't understand, then the strain on his arms resumed, and once more he felt himself being dragged. He was dropped unceremoniously, and he could smell the stink of sour water; probably from one of the troughs that lined the street. He opened his eyes for a split second, and saw Rattigan lean over him to grab for the Colt.

Another shot was fired, this time sending a slug into the water-softened wood of the trough. Slocum heard the slap of water recoiling from the impact of the bullet, and some water splattered his face.

He was forced to close his eyes again, and he scrambled to his knees, groping blindly for the trough. When he found it, he leaned over, scooped water into both hands and splashed his face. Gunfire exploded just to his right, not more than eighteen inches away, and he felt a hand pressing on his back. Shaking it off, he splashed his face again, then plunged his head into the sour water of the horse trough, opened his eyes, and blinked several times until the sand was washed away.

Spluttering, he straightened up and opened his eyes. Through blurred vision, he saw Rattigan kneeling beside him, still pulling the trigger on the Colt, although it was empty by now, and the hammer kept clicking on empty shells.

The big Irishman's shoulder was stained dark red, and an ugly crease in both his shoulder and his shirt gaped open where a bullet had narrowly missed striking bone. Reaching for the Colt, Slocum asked, "Did you get a good look at them?"

"Oh yeah, I got a good look all right."

Slocum broke the Navy open, extracted the empty rounds, then reached for some fresh ammunition from his gun belt. Wiping his eyes on his sleeve, he reloaded, jerked the pistol closed, and holstered it. He glanced toward the far end of town, but the gunmen were gone. A cloud of dust hung in the early evening sunlight.

Slocum saw people running, then, as his vision cleared still further, he realized someone else had been wounded. A man lay in the street on his back. Even through the watery haze that clouded his sight, Slocum could see that the man had been hit twice. Like Rattigan, he had taken a bullet in the shoulder, and it looked as if he had also been hit in the left leg above the knee. Two pools of blood had spread out on the dirt beside him, but he was still alive, and kept trying to sit up.

"You all right, Phil?" Slocum asked.

Before Rattigan could answer, Maggie Carson came running through the restaurant door and out into the street. "My God, Phil, you've been shot!" she screamed. "Help, help us, somebody!"

"Hush yourself, woman," Rattigan barked. "It's nothing—just a crease. I don't think Jason Bridge's been so lucky, though."

Maggie glanced up the street, saw the wounded man, and covered her face with her hands. "Lord Jesus, not again," she said, "not again. I can't stand this anymore. I just can't stand it."

Slocum got to his feet and helped Rattigan up, who ignored the pain of his wound and put his uninjured arm around Maggie Carson. "Slocum, you better see to Jason," he said. "I'll get Maggie inside and be there directly."

Slocum nodded. "You sure?"

"I'm sure." Without waiting for an argument, he half pulled and half carried Maggie up onto the boardwalk and on through the open doorway of the Silver Skillet. Slocum started up the street, noticing that the crowd was hardly that, maybe seven or eight people, including the large, round storekeeper with the impressive mustache, who had taken off his apron and was knotting it around the wounded man's leg.

The onlookers paid Slocum just enough attention to move out of his way. He looked at their faces for a moment, and knew the glazed look only too well. They were scared, but they were also fascinated. There was something about death, or its near proximity, that seemed to transfix people and freeze their faces into a kind of dumb amazement.

"Can I help?" Slocum asked.

The merchant looked up. "Not unless you're a doctor. Jason needs somebody to tend to these wounds here. He's bleeding pretty bad."

"Is there a doctor in town?"

"Somebody went to fetch him, but odds are he's got a snootful of whiskey and likely won't be much help until he sobers up."

"What about the law?"

The merchant glared at him then. "What about it?"

"There a sheriff?"

The fat man shrugged. "Yes and no," he said.

"What the hell's that supposed to mean?" Slocum jerked a large handkerchief from his pocket and knelt down beside the merchant. He wrapped the handkerchief around the wound in the man's shoulder, then tied it off just tight enough to stop the bleeding. It was a clean shot, through and through, and the wound wasn't bleeding badly enough to suggest it had severed an artery.

The fat man finally answered the question. "It means there is a sheriff and there ain't one. That's pretty plain."

"Not to me."

"Well, after you been here a while, maybe you'll understand. Looked to me like them boys wouldn't have minded putting a couple of bullet holes in your hide, no more than they minded plugging Jason, here." He looked at Slocum hard for a moment. "Why do you suppose that is?"

"Your guess is as good as mine."

"It is, is it?"

"That's what I said," Slocum barked.

The fat man recoiled a few inches, as if afraid Slocum might bite him, and then he held his hands up placatingly. "Now take it easy, I didn't mean nothing. I just . . ." He trailed off, leaving Slocum to fill in the blanks.

Hearing heavy footsteps behind him, Slocum turned to see Phil Rattigan racing toward him.

"How is he?" the bartender shouted. "He all right?"

Bridge was out cold, probably from shock and the loss of blood. "He took two, but I think he'll be all right if we can get him stitched up."

"Probably have to pour a gallon of coffee down Doc Abernathy's miserable craw before he can do anything. Otherwise, he's likely to sew his own hand over the bullet hole."

The merchant laughed, and Rattigan shook his head. "Never seen the like of that man, thank the good Lord," he said.

"What about the sheriff?" Slocum asked.

Rattigan wrinkled his nose. "Be kind of like throwing kerosene on a fire," he said.

"I wish somebody would tell me what the hell is going on here."

Rattigan clapped him on the shoulder using his wounded arm, and winced. "Don't make no difference, Slocum. You're moving on in the morning. No sense in worryin' about something don't concern you."

"Listen, Phil, when somebody takes a shot at me, it concerns me. Don't you think?"

Rattigan shrugged.

"You saw them. Who were they?"

"What difference does it make?"

"Who were they?" Slocum raised his voice, and Rattigan frowned.

"Ray Sadler and some of the other Broken C boys."

"You have any idea why they wanted to shoot this man?" Slocum asked, pointing to the unconscious Jason Bridge.

"Sure he does." It was the storekeeper speaking. "So do I. Tom Childress don't like competition, is why. And Jason don't like to be pushed, so when Childress and his men started to shove, Jason shoved right back. Damn near got hisself killed. Most likely, they'll keep on tryin' until they get it done right."

"Why?"

"You really want to know?" Rattigan asked.

"Damn right I do," Slocum said.

"Well, I guess you got reason. I'll—"

"Look out, there, let me through. . . ."

Rattigan said, "That'll be Doc Abernathy. Let's get Jason tended to, then I'll tell you whatever you want to know."

The small crowd, swollen now to more than a dozen and a half, parted again. A small man with a paunch and a shock of unruly white hair draped over a florid forehead made his way through and knelt down. He had a black bag that he dropped without ceremony, and opened without looking.

"Stand back and let me have a look at this man, will you? For Christ's sake, you're like a pack of buzzards. Go on, get out of here." Abernathy waved his arms wildly, and the people backed away, but only far enough to keep out of the doctor's reach.

Reaching into the bag, he found a scalpel in a small leather case. He removed it, and slit Bridge's pant leg and the apron tied over it to expose the wound.

"Un, um, um. That's ugly," he said.

"He gonna pull through, Doc?" Rattigan asked.

"Hell, I don't know—but he's got a damn sight better chance if you leave me be. Phil, why don't you chase the rest of these worthless coyotes out of here and get this man to my office, where I can do a decent job of it?"

"You got it Doc," Rattigan said. "Give me a hand, Slocum."

They grabbed Bridge by either end, Slocum taking him by the ankles and Rattigan taking him by the shoulders, and started to trudge up the street, while Abernathy led the way, waving his medical bag as if it were a weapon. "Go on home, worthless idiots. Go on home and leave me be."

Abernathy's office was up a flight of rickety stairs, and negotiating the two turns with the limp form of Jason Bridge was anything but easy. Rattigan's wound had been wrapped in a makeshift bandage, and Slocum could see blood seeping through the cloth as the big man strained against the dead weight wrapped in his bearlike embrace.

"Better let the Doc look at your arm, Phil," Slocum suggested.

"You trying to kill me?" Rattigan said, gritting his teeth.

Abernathy, opening the door to his office, said, "Don't delude yourself, Rattigan. A man with twice my skill couldn't rid the world of you."

4

Jason Bridge was pale. Weak from the loss of blood, he seemed not to know where he was as Abernathy bandaged the wound in his thigh.

"You're one lucky fella," Abernathy said. "Half inch to the left, and that bullet would have ripped a hole in an artery. You'd have bled to death for sure."

Bridge managed a weak smile. His fair complexion, bleached by the trauma, was sprinkled with freckles the same color as his reddish-brown hair. Green eyes peered out from the white mask, frightened and darting. "Always was lucky, Doc," he said. "Ever since I was a kid, back in Pennsylvania."

"Maybe you should have stayed there," Abernathy suggested. "Don't imagine folks shoot up the town much back east, do they, Jason?"

Slocum sat quietly on a cane chair in the corner while Abernathy finished his work. He was watching Jason Bridge closely, and what he saw was an ordinary man, a man who had come into town to buy groceries and, for reasons that no one seemed to want to talk about, had almost been killed. He was curious, and he was angry, angry at the senselessness of it, and angrier still that he had been sucked into the middle of something he didn't understand.

Waiting for Phil Rattigan, who had gone to get the town sheriff, he kept his own counsel, but he had a few questions, and before he moved on, he wanted a few answers.

A heavy step on the creaky wooden stairs leading up to the doctor's office signaled an approach. He heard Rattigan's voice, his mellow baritone was reduced to a whisper, as if he didn't want to be overheard. The door opened, and Rattigan stepped into the pale orange light of a kerosene lamp, then he stepped aside, and held the screen door open.

The man who followed Rattigan inside was as lean as a whippet. His angular face seemed composed of shards of pottery stuck together with more haste than geometry, and fired to a dull bronze. A black mustache drooped under a pair of the blackest eyes Slocum had ever seen, and a lock of jet-black hair dangled over a broad forehead.

"Doc," he said, "what you got here?"

"Sheriff," Abernathy answered, "what's it look like I got? A shooting. Jason here almost got his ticket punched for sure."

The sheriff noticed Slocum then, and glanced at him with flat, snakelike eyes. "Who's he?" he asked Abernathy.

Rattigan answered. "That's John Slocum, fella I told you about. He was there when the shooting started."

The sheriff nodded, stepped around the table where Bridge now lay with his eyes closed and his teeth clenched, and stuck out a veiny hand. "Slocum," he said, "name's Walter Kennedy, Sheriff of Las Cruces."

Slocum shook the offered hand. "Sheriff, pleased to meet you."

Turning then to the patient, the sheriff said, "You have any idea what this is all about, Slocum?"

"None."

"How come you're here, then?"

"When people shoot at me, I take it personally."

"You know who done it?"

"Yeah, I do. I don't know all the names, but I know where to find them."

Kennedy pushed his hat back on his forehead, allowing a cascade of jet-black hair to spill over his brow. "How you happen to know these men?"

"I don't actually know them, I just know who they are."

"Hold on, Sheriff," Phil Rattigan said, "I already told you what happened. What are you badgering Slocum for?"

The sheriff sighed with exasperation. "Because, Mister Rattigan, when there's a shooting, and somebody I never laid eyes on just happens to be in the middle of it, I get a little curious. I want to know what happened, and maybe, just maybe, Slocum knows something I don't. I ask him questions, he answers them, and then I see where things stand."

"He wasn't in the middle of it, Sheriff. He was in the Silver Skillet with me when the shooting started. He went outside, and Ray Sadler and a

few of the Broken C boys started shooting at him.
They'd already hit Jason."

Kennedy looked at Slocum. "That how it happened?"

Slocum nodded.

"How come you stuck your nose in where it don't
belong? Some sort of avenging angel? You always
do that sort of thing, do you?"

"Not always, no," Slocum said.

"Why this time?"

Slocum shrugged. "Look, Sheriff, I'll tell you one
more time . . . when the shooting started, I went
outside to see what was happening. The men who
shot Mister Bridge turned their guns on me. I got
sand in my eyes, and I couldn't see very well. In
fact, if it hadn't have been for Mister Rattigan, I'd
probably be lying there next to Mister Bridge. You
asked me who, and I told you. Don't bother to ask
me why, because I don't know. I had a little run-in
with Ray Sadler at Rattigan's Saloon earlier. He
was drunk, and maybe he figured he had a score
to settle. He saw me and started shooting. But that
doesn't explain why he shot Mister Bridge, and it
seems to me like that's the question you ought to
try to answer."

"Are you Sheriff here now? Is that it? I lost my
job and nobody bothered to tell me, is that what
happened?"

Slocum shrugged. "All I'm saying is, if it's your
job, why in hell don't you do it, instead of asking
me a bunch of pointless questions? You know who's
responsible for the shooting. Arrest them."

"Now that's where you're wrong, Mister Slocum.
I may know who *done* the shooting, if I can believe

what you and Rattigan tell me, but—"

"Wait a minute, Sheriff," Rattigan interrupted. "Are you saying you don't believe me?"

Kennedy glared at him, but didn't respond. "As I was saying, I may know who *done* the shooting, but that don't mean I know who's responsible."

"You won't find that out standing here asking stupid questions!" Rattigan exploded. "Jesus Christ, Sheriff. A man was almost murdered. Why don't you do your job?"

"I will, Mister Rattigan. It's what I get paid for, and I will do it. But you'll have to leave it to me to decide how it's best done."

He turned to Bridge again, and this time leaned forward. "Mister Bridge," he said, "do you have any idea who shot you?"

"No, I don't."

Slocum was stunned. He looked at Rattigan, whose baffled expression was evidence he had no idea what was going on.

"You see the men who shot you, did you?"

"Sort of, but not clear enough that I could identify any of 'em. It all happened so fast. I just don't know. . . ."

Kennedy sucked on a tooth, and looked at Slocum. Nodding, he said, "You see what I mean, Slocum? Things ain't always as cut and dried as folks want to believe. Mister Bridge don't seem to know who shot him. You're a stranger here in town, and I got no reason to believe or disbelieve anything you tell me, but I got to wonder how you come to know Ray Sadler's name. I also got to wonder why a man I know for years would have reason to want to kill you. And even if Sadler did shoot at you, that don't mean he's the one who shot at Mister Bridge. You see my problem?"

"No, I don't." He looked at Rattigan for support. "Mister Rattigan saw the men better than I did, but he told you the same thing. He knows Sadler, and he saw what happened."

The Sheriff turned to Rattigan. "Did you see Ray Sadler shoot Mister Bridge, Phil?"

Rattigan shook his head. "Not actually, I mean Jason was already hit by the time I come out, and—"

"So, are you telling me you didn't see Bridge get shot?"

Rattigan took a long breath, held it, then squeezed it out between compressed lips. "Yeah, I'm telling you I didn't actually *see* Jason get shot, but—"

"There you are, then," Kennedy interrupted. "Not much I can do about the shooting of Mister Bridge here, without some investigating. As to Mister Slocum, well, maybe you just walked into the middle of something without seeing what was going on. Maybe Ray Sadler wasn't shooting at you at all. Maybe he was shooting at whoever shot Mister Bridge, and you just accidentally got caught in the middle."

"That's not what happened, Sheriff."

"So you tell me, but I can't go around arresting people without cause. I got to know what happened. What I got here is this. I got a man who's been shot, but don't know who shot him. I got a man who says he knows who shot the first man, but he didn't see it happen, and I got a third man who says *he* knows what happened and who done it, but he had sand in his eyes so he didn't really see nothing at all. You see how it is? How'm I gonna get a judge to convict anybody on that sort of testimony?"

"Does that mean you're not gonna do anything?" Rattigan demanded.

"Now, I didn't say that. Of course I'll do something, but I got to look into this carefully. I can't go off half cocked."

"What you mean," Rattigan said, "is that you have to check with Tom Childress to see what he'll let you do. Isn't that right, Sheriff?"

Kennedy bristled. "This don't have nothing to do with Mister Childress. I ain't heard his name mentioned in this till now, so I don't see why you'd even suggest something like that."

"Don't you?"

"Are you telling me you think Tom Childress shot Jason Bridge?"

Rattigan snorted. "Jesus Christ, why do I even bother?" he waved a hand in disgust, and turned his back.

The sheriff looked at Slocum. "I'd appreciate it, Mister Slocum, if you'd make yourself available for a couple of days. I might need to talk to you again."

"Actually, I was planning to move on, Sheriff. And the fact of the matter is, it doesn't seem like there's any reason for me to hang around."

"There sure as hell is a reason. I'm tellin' you to. That good enough for you, or do I have to slap you in jail?"

Slocum took a deep breath and clenched his fists as he slowly exhaled. "I guess it'll have to be, won't it?"

"Damn right," Kennedy said. He touched the brim of his hat and moved toward the door. "Gents," he said, "I'll be in touch."

When he was gone, Rattigan exploded. "That goddamned weasel," he said. "He knows exactly what happened, and he won't do a goddamned thing about it." Angrily, he turned on Jason Bridge. "Why in hell didn't you tell him what happened? Why didn't you tell him it was Ray Sadler?"

Bridge gave a wan smile. "You saw what happened. You think it would have made any difference what I said?" He tried to get up, but when his legs dangled over the table, he started to wobble, and nearly lost his balance. "Got to get home," he said.

"You're too weak to be goin' anywhere," Doc Abernathy said. "Least ways, by yourself."

"I got stuff in the wagon. Sarah will wonder where I am. She'll worry."

"I'll take you home," Slocum offered.

Bridge shook his head. "No need for you to get mixed up in this, Mister Slocum."

"Looks like I already am."

5

There was barely enough room for Jason Bridge in the back of his wagon. Rattigan and Slocum had carried him down as if he was a sack of grain, then placed him on the wagon bed with a borrowed blanket from Doc Abernathy folded beneath him to cushion the hard boards a bit.

Rattigan had to get back to his saloon, so Slocum tethered his horse to the rear of the wagon, then climbed up into the seat. It had been a while since he'd driven a wagon, and he didn't much care for it, but there was no alternative and he decided to make the best of it.

He wanted to know a little more about Sheriff Kennedy, and a lot more about Tom Childress and Ray Sadler, but he'd have to wait until he got a chance to see Rattigan again. There was little more than a half hour before sundown, but Rattigan had assured him that the Bridge ranch was easy to find.

"Besides," the big Irishman had said, "there's gonna be a full moon tonight, almost, and if you can't find your way five or six miles, then maybe you ought to be turned out to pasture."

Bridge was so weak, he kept drifting off to sleep, but then would wake up with a start and ask where he was, so Slocum was on his own once he left the edge of Las Cruces behind him.

In the back of his mind was the thought that Sadler might be out there somewhere waiting for him, but it seemed unlikely, and he shrugged it off. The only concession to that possibility was the Winchester carbine laying on the seat beside him. Its butt was wedged in behind his own just to make sure it didn't slide around as the wagon bounced and rattled over the rutted road.

Once, he thought he saw someone watching him off to the south against a line of pines, but the failing light was too imprecise for him to be sure. And the last thing he wanted to do was spend the next couple of days jumping at shadows. Still, he kept a watchful eye on the trees for a quarter of a mile.

Slocum wasn't happy about staying on in Las Cruces, but there wasn't a hell of a lot he could do about it. He had a bit of a shady past, and he didn't need Kennedy poking around in it. It was enough that he'd let the sheriff know he thought him a fool and an incompetent. That Rattigan had added the possibility Kennedy might be bought and paid for with Broken C money was more insulting still, but the sheriff had seemed less incensed by the innuendo than he might have. And that did little to ease Slocum's concerns.

The sun went down so abruptly, it seemed as if someone had leaned over and blown it out. For a moment, it was pitch black, and then the sky seemed to explode into streaks of gold and purple. Heavy masses of clouds were backlit by the setting sun, and their edges glowed bright orange, as if they had been trimmed with paint.

The second light faded, and soon the road ahead of him was pale gray against the darker gray of the tall grass on either side. It was easy enough to follow, and with Jason Bridge lying in the back of the wagon, there was no temptation to really push the team. Clucking now and then to the horses, Slocum kept the reins coiled in one fist, occasionally snapping them to keep the animals moving at a steady pace.

He'd gone a little over three and a half miles when everything started to turn silver. The moon was coming up sooner than he'd expected, and soon the sky changed color, its deep blue-black taking on a little more blue. Shadowed by the hills beyond it, the tree line to the south was closer to the road now, and looked like a vein of coal between the silver of the grass and the wash of the moonlight.

Ten minutes later, he spotted a point of light that appeared to be almost dead center in the road at least a mile or so ahead. In the moonlight, he couldn't be sure, but that had to be the Bridge place, he thought. He kept his eye on the light now, waiting for it to grow larger, but it was still too far away to show any change as the wagon continued to shudder and bang over the packed earth of the ruts.

The drive seemed to take forever, but soon the dim outline of a house emerged from the darkness.

There was light in three windows, and he could see that the front door was open. Off to one side, the bulk of a barn loomed against the sky, looking solid as a rock, almost as if it had been carved from black stone.

He turned to see if Jason Bridge was awake; he wanted to tell him the agonizing ride was almost over, but the wounded man was still sleeping. Sensing they were near home, the horses sped up, and Slocum had to tighten the reins on them to keep them from bolting.

He could see a fence now, split rail from the look of it, and then a gate, open and leaning a bit, but solid looking. The horses made the turn without any help from him, and as the clatter of the wagon reached the house, he saw the rectangle of light in the doorway suddenly blocked by an indistinct figure.

He wasn't sure whether it was a man or a woman, but he recognized the instrument in the figure's hands as a shotgun. He didn't doubt that it was loaded. Slowing the wagon, he called, "Hello there. . . ."

"Who are you, and what do you want?"

The lilt of the voice was decidedly feminine, but the razor edge of the words let him know he'd better answer or find out what gauge shot she'd loaded.

"Name's Slocum. You Sarah Bridge?"

She nodded. Then, realizing that he couldn't see her that clearly, she said, "That's right. What do you want here?"

"Your husband's been hurt Ma'am—shot in town this afternoon."

She rushed out of the house then with a little cry like that of a frightened bird, the steel suddenly gone dull. "Oh my God! Jason. Where is he? What . . . ?"

"Now hold on," Slocum said. "I've got him here in the wagon. He's weak, but he'll be all right. Lost a lot of blood, though."

He braked the wagon, fearful that he might run her down in the narrow lane, and as she raced past him, she flashed him a glare that would wither a redwood, as if he'd done the shooting.

He felt the wagon shift as she climbed over the tailgate. "Jason," she said. "Jason, it's Sarah. Wake up, Jason, wake up." There was a frantic edge to the request, almost as if she feared he might be dead.

Bridge groaned, and started to mumble something. Then, as if for the first time realizing something was wrong, he said, "Sarah, what happened? What are you doing here?"

"You've been hurt, Jason. You've been shot. Oh my God!"

"I know," he said. "I know."

"It was that bastard Ray Sadler, wasn't it? That whole mob of them ought to—" She caught herself as Slocum turned in the seat. Realizing she didn't know who, or what, he was, she didn't finish.

"We better get him inside," Slocum suggested. "He's been through hell this afternoon. Hang on, I'm going to pull the wagon up to the front porch." Without waiting for an argument, he released the brake, snapped the reins, and clucked to the team.

When the wagon lurched into motion, Sarah Bridge nearly lost her balance and was forced to grab hold of Slocum's shoulder to stay upright. She knelt then, hastily withdrawing her hand and grabbing hold of the side of the wagon.

Pulling into the front yard, Slocum maneuvered the wagon alongside the porch so the tailgate was just past the three steps leading up to the house. Setting the brake and knotting the reins around the handle, he jumped down and moved toward the rear of the wagon.

Jason Bridge tried to get out of the wagon without help, but the effort of dragging himself to the tailgate sapped whatever strength he had, and he doubled over gasping for breath. Sarah slid off the wagon bed and turned her body so Jason could drape an arm across her shoulders. Slocum took a similar position on the opposite side.

"Ready?" he asked.

Jason Bridge nodded. Slocum took the major portion of the wounded man's weight, and straightened up as Jason let his feet feel for the ground. Getting him up the steps was going to be the toughest part. Taking it one step at a time, the ungainly trio negotiated the ascent. Sarah leaned forward to yank open the screen door, then extended one booted foot to hold it aside until Jason was through the doorway.

"Where do you want him?" Slocum asked.

Sarah nodded toward a doorway and said, "In back, in his bedroom." They turned sideways, and like an awkward insect uncertain how to synchronize its half dozen legs, they stumbled down the hall to a door on the left.

Sarah went in first, and in the dim light Slocum could just discern the outline of a bed across the room under an open window. The moonlight spilling in through lace curtains filled the room with shades of gray. When they were close enough, Sarah let go, and watched as Slocum lowered Jason to the bed. The wounded man knelt on the cover, leaned over, then collapsed face down.

Sarah struggled to get him under the heavy bedspread, then turned her efforts to lighting a kerosene lamp on a table at the head of the bed. The flame fluttered until she lowered the glass chimney into place, then settled into a steady glow.

Jason was already asleep.

Slocum backed out of the room, thinking he ought to give Sarah some time alone with Jason, but she followed him out and closed the door.

"Who are you?" she demanded.

Taken aback by the abruptness of the question, Slocum stammered, "Name's John Slocum, Misses Bridge. I just—"

"Miss," she snapped.

"Pardon?"

"I said it's Miss. Jason is my brother, not my husband."

"Oh, sorry, I didn't—"

"Who are you?" she interrupted. "What in heaven's name is going on here? Who shot my brother, and why?"

Slocum took a deep breath. "I've been wondering what's going on myself, Ma'am, but I have to confess that I'm as much in the dark as anybody."

"It was Ray Sadler, wasn't it? That damned Tom Childress won't rest until he puts Jason in his grave."

"Well," Slocum said, "you're right about one thing. It was Ray Sadler and some of his cronies. I know that much for certain, even though I can't get Sheriff Kennedy to do anything about it."

Sarah snorted. "Sheriff Kennedy? You must be joking. If Tom Childress wants something from his pocket, he's got to push Walt Kennedy aside to get at it."

"I got somewhat the same story from Phil Rattigan," Slocum said.

She looked at him hard, as if she suspected he might be trying to get inside her defenses. "You still didn't tell me how you're involved in all this. Who are you, just some Good Samaritan, is that what you expect me to believe?"

"I don't expect you to believe much of anything, Miss Bridge, and frankly, I don't give a good goddamn what you think. Your brother was hurt and I offered to help out. Now, if that rates as a high crime in this part of New Mexico, I'm sorry. Where I come from, it's just being neighborly." He tipped his hat and turned for the door.

"Wait, Mister Slocum . . . I . . . I'm sorry. I didn't mean to . . ." Her lips trembled, but no further sound escaped them.

Slocum stood there looking at her over his shoulder. "Miss Bridge, there's something going on here that I don't know about. But whatever it is, it almost got your brother killed, and it almost got me killed right along with him. Now, if you want to tell me what's really happening around here, maybe I can help some. Lord knows, I wouldn't mind twisting Ray Sadler's tail into a knot or two.

But I'm out on a lake without an oar, and it's a long way back to shore."

Sarah rubbed her hands on her thighs and let the tip of her tongue slide across her upper lip. "I'm so confused," she said. "So scared. I'm scared to death, and there's not a damn thing I can do about it."

"Don't be so sure," he said, taking a step toward the dining table and pulling up a chair. "Tell me everything."

6

Sarah poured a cup of coffee and pushed it across the table toward Slocum. "Sugar?" she asked.

Slocum shook his head. "Black's fine."

Sarah poured a second cup for herself, returned the pot to the fireplace, then sat at the table across from him, cradling the cup of coffee in her hands as if trying to warm them. "What do you want to know?" she asked.

"For starters, I'd like to know why Ray Sadler wants your brother dead."

"I don't think it's Ray Sadler so much as Tom Childress."

"Tell me about that. His name keeps coming up and everybody seems to have something they want to say, but can't manage to spit out."

"Tom Childress owns almost all of this valley. He's been building an empire here ever since he arrived, as near as I can tell. A lot of people don't like him, so I guess maybe you have to discount what they say, but from what I've heard, there have been a number of small ranchers driven out

43

of this part of New Mexico in the last few years. Some sold out, some were burned out, and some just turned up dead."

"And Childress was the buyer?"

"Always."

"And the law hasn't bothered him about the arson or the deaths?"

"Tom Childress is the law—if there is any in Las Cruces. I told you before that Walter Kennedy is as much his as if Childress bought him at an auction, like he did a few of the ranches he's acquired."

"And where does your brother fit in?"

"Childress has been trying to buy Jason out for nearly a year. Jason won't even talk to him about it, and Childress has been looking for some excuse to cause trouble. Last month, though, things seemed to come to a head. Jason bid on the army contract to supply horses to Fort Stanton. Childress bid, too, but Jason won the contract."

"So Childress gets rid of Jason and he solves two problems with one funeral. Is that how you see it?"

Sarah bristled. "Yes, that's how I see it. I don't think there's any other way *to* see it. But it doesn't matter now, anyhow."

"Why not?"

"Because the first delivery of horses is due in five days. Fifty head. Jason'll never be able to make that delivery, not in the shape he's in."

"Maybe you can get an extension."

Sarah shook her head. "I don't think so. The contract was quite explicit: all deliveries had to be made on time. Failure to make any delivery voids the contract. And if that delivery isn't made, we lose the contract and the ranch goes, too. There's a mortgage payment due the first of the month—that's in eight days. Without payment from the army, we default, and the bank forecloses."

"Maybe the bank can be—"

"No. Childress owns the bank, or at least he owns Tyler Hutchins, who owns the bank. It's all the same."

"So Childress doesn't even need Jason dead, does he? All he needs is what he's got; Jason laid up long enough to miss the delivery date, and he gets the army contract and your ranch."

"That's right." Sarah was almost defiant, but it was a struggle, and Slocum could sense that she felt like she was teetering on the edge of a yawning precipice. If she lost her balance, she would fall, and once she fell, there would be no climbing back out of the abyss.

"You don't have any hired help?" he asked.

Sarah shook her head. Setting the coffee cup down with a sharp crack, she said, "Me and Jason work the ranch, and I can't afford to hire anybody. Besides, everybody around here is scared of Childress and Sadler. They know what could happen if they helped us out. No, it's hopeless." She buried her face in her hands, and her shoulders shook, but she made no sound.

Slocum reached across the table and pried her hands loose. She fought him for a moment, then allowed him to have his way. She looked up when he chucked her under the chin. The tears made her eyes a brilliant shade of blue that seemed, if anything, deeper than a mountain lake. They were the most beautiful eyes he'd ever seen. The sprinkling of freckles across the bridge of her nose did nothing to detract from them, nor did her full lips.

"There is one thing that might work," Slocum said.

She brightened momentarily, then lapsed back into gloom, like a drowning woman who saw the last lifeline fall short. She said nothing.

"Don't you want to know what it is?" he asked.

"You'll tell me anyway, won't you?"

Slocum laughed. "I'm out of a job. I could help you get the horses in, and drive them to Fort Stanton."

"I already told you, we can't afford to hire anyone."

"I work cheap. All I need are meals and a place to stay. Kennedy told me to stay around for a few days, and since I always abide by the wishes of the law," he grinned, "I might just as well find something to do. Idle hands, and all that. . . ."

Sarah looked doubtful. "I don't know. How much do you know about horses?"

Slocum looked offended. "You think maybe I'm a dentist, Miss Bridge?" He held out his callused hands. "Do these look like a preacher's hands?"

Sarah took a long time as she sipped her coffee, and watched Slocum over the rim of the mug. When she finally set it down on the table, she kept her slender fingers curled around it. "Why?"

"I don't understand the question."

"Why would you want to help us? You don't know us. You have no reason to care what happens to us. If what you say is true, you never laid eyes on either one of us before today. So . . . why?"

"Maybe I'm stubborn. Maybe I'm a champion of lost causes. Maybe it galls me to see two decent people squashed under the boot heels of a man like Tom Childress . . . there are a lot of reasons. The important thing is that the offer is genuine. You need help getting those horses rounded up, and I'm willing to do it for room and board. There's not much in my pocket at the moment, and. . . ." He spread his hands as if helpless to make his reasons any more persuasive. "Besides, what have you got to lose?"

She smiled then, her face almost radiant in the lamplight. She took a deep breath, once more traced the fleshy contours of her mouth with the tip of her tongue. "It really ought to be up to Jason."

"Jason's sleeping. Time is running out, and if Jason says no because he's stubborn or frightened, then you'll lose the one chance you have to meet the delivery deadline. As it is, you might not make it, but it costs you nothing to try."

"All right," she nodded her head, tilting it slightly as if listening to a voice from another room. "All right, but on one condition."

"What?"

"If we do make it, you'll allow us to pay you something for your trouble. It may not be much, but I can't allow you to do it for nothing more than a bed in the barn and a mouthful of food. We don't want charity, don't need it, and won't accept it."

"Agreed."

"All right then. We'll start first thing in the morning."

"I'll tend to the wagon and the team," Slocum said.

"I want to look in on Jason. When you're finished, I'll get you some bedding and, oh, I suppose you must be hungry . . . ?"

"As a matter of fact, Phil Rattigan and I were just sitting down at the Silver Skillet when the shooting started. So, yes, I'm hungry. Hungry enough to eat a horse, in fact, but I don't suppose that's something we can afford to do at the moment."

She laughed for the first time, a resonant, husky sound that made him smile. "No," she said, "I don't suppose we can afford that. But I'll get something else ready for you. I'm no Maggie Carson, but it'll be edible, at least. Come in when you're finished."

Slocum reached across the table with one hand extended. Sarah looked at it for a moment with bewilderment, then, realizing what he meant, she shook his hand. Her fingers felt cool against his palm, and he squeezed. She returned the pressure, and he felt in her hand the same resilient steel he'd heard in her voice when he first arrived.

Excusing himself, he went outside. The team was shuffling restlessly, and when he climbed up into the wagon seat, they bobbed their heads nervously. At first he thought they were simply anxious to move, but then he felt compelled to look around, and peered into the shadowy corners over near the barn. For a moment, he thought he saw something move. He climbed down from the wagon, then reached back into the seat for the Winchester as an afterthought.

He walked toward the barn cautiously, and leaned forward slightly, to try and see through the darkness. The barn seemed almost to glow in the moonlight, as if it were sheathed in shiny pewter. When he reached the door, he noticed it was open a foot; not much, but enough to allow someone to slip inside.

Grabbing the door by its edge, he yanked it open, and jumped back almost by instinct. The hinges creaked, but no other sound came from the cavernous interior. It was pitch black inside, and he crept to the wall to peer in. "Hello? Anyone there?"

His own voice came back to him, and he heard the skitter of something in the straw that was too small to be anything more than a mouse. He wished he had a lantern, but was reluctant to light a match to look for one. If someone was inside, the glow would make Slocum a perfect target. Listening for a long moment, he decided it was nothing, just his nerves on edge, and he relaxed.

Walking back to the wagon, he refused the temptation to glance back over his shoulder. "Easy, Slocum," he whispered, "don't get spooked."

Climbing back onto the wagon, he laid the Winchester across his lap, unlooped the reins, and released the brake. Turning the wagon around, he urged the team toward the black opening in the barn side, snapped the reins once or twice, and drove on inside. Then he jumped down, walked to the wall, and felt along the door frame on the left side until he felt the cold metal of a lantern reservoir.

Once he had the lantern lit, he felt better. Unhitching the team, he led them outside and put them in a corral. He unsaddled his own mount, led the big gray outside, and also turned him loose in the corral. Then he forked some hay from the loft. Back on the ground floor, he retrieved his rifle and walked back to the house.

Sarah had a plate heaped with stew and a fresh cup of coffee all ready for him. On a chair beside the table, he saw two folded blankets.

"All finished?" she asked.

Slocum nodded. "Ready for supper, boss."

He pulled out a chair, sat down, and bellied up to the table. He noticed that there was no plate across from him. "You've eaten already?" he asked.

"Yes," she said. Then, after hesitating, she added, "Actually, that's a lie. I just don't feel like eating— but you go ahead. There's more, if you want it."

Slocum dug in. The stew was hot, and he liked the taste enough to wipe the plate clean with a hunk of fresh bread. He washed it down with the last of his coffee. When he was finished, Sarah cleared the table, grabbed the blankets, which she held across her chest folded in both arms, and said, "Let's get you set for the night."

She walked outside and looked up at the moon for a moment before stepping off the porch and walking to the barn. He'd left the lantern lit, and when he followed her inside, he saw her look around. She wrinkled her nose, and said, "I wish we could offer you better accommodations, but. . . ."

"This'll do, Miss Bridge."

She held out the blankets, and he walked to a pile of straw, rearranged it with the toe of one boot, and spread a blanket on top of it for a makeshift mattress. He left the other one folded, and set it on top of the first. When he turned around, she was so close his elbow rubbed against her hip. "Good night," he said.

"Good night, Mister Slocum."

He turned back to the improvised bed, and her hand closed on his shoulder. She squeezed it gently. "Thank you," she said.

7

The morning dawned crisp and clear. It was the middle of September, and the sunlight seemed to lend everything an abnormal clarity, creating a sense of distance, as if Slocum was looking at objects through a sheet of glass. He washed up at the pump, then walked to the house. The door was still closed and locked. He rapped twice, then listened for some movement. His pocket watch showed the time as six-thirty, and he wondered whether Sarah Bridge was even awake yet. But as soon as the thought crossed his mind, he heard the rap of boot heels on wood beyond the door.

The door swung back and she stood there with her hands on her hips. "It's about time you woke up," she said. "It's a good thing I didn't agree to pay you a weekly wage." But she smiled, and Slocum, after a moment of uncertainty, knew she was just teasing him.

She stepped outside, and he noticed that her eyes were puffy and red, as if she'd been crying. But she was dressed for work with a pair of jeans hugging her hips and outlining long, well-muscled legs. She wore a loose-fitting denim shirt, but despite the slackness of the cloth, he found himself staring at her ample chest for just a split second longer than politeness dictated. She noticed, but didn't seem to mind.

"I hope you don't object to a cold breakfast," she said. "I didn't want to bother with a fire, since we wouldn't be here very long."

"Cold beans'll do," Slocum said. "How's your brother doing?"

"He slept all night. He was awake for a while this morning, but he's sleeping again now."

"Does he know what we're planning to do?"

"I told him. He didn't seem happy with the idea, but he agreed. He knows it's our only chance. Hurry and eat, we've got a good ride before we get to the horses." She held the door for him, then followed him inside. Once again, she sat across from him while he ate a breakfast that was more filling than tasty. He settled for a cup of cold water, since coffee was out of the question.

"Where are the horses?" Slocum asked.

"About two hours ride, up in the hills. We had already started to round them up, but we have to supply at least fifty head, and we'd only managed twenty-odd. And we have to brand them with that ugly US the army uses."

Slocum pushed away from the table. "Let's get moving," he said.

Sarah went out to the corral ahead of him, and Slocum followed her. While he saddled the big gray, Sarah saddled her own mount, a sorrel stallion with intelligent eyes and a feisty manner. They were

ready before seven. Slocum slid his Winchester
into its boot and swung up into the saddle. He
noticed that Sarah's boot was empty.

"You have a rifle?" he asked.

She nodded.

"Can you use it?"

Again, she shook her head affirmatively.

"Better get it, then," he said. "I don't expect trouble, but if it comes, we want to be ready. Two guns
are always better than one."

Sarah ran back to the house and reappeared
with a new Springfield carbine and a box of ammunition. She booted the Springfield, swung up onto
the sorrel, and tucked the box of bullets into one
of her saddlebags. "I guess we're ready," she said.

"Lead the way."

It was a long ride. Las Cruces was at the center
of a huge, bowl-shaped valley. It was ideal for
ranching with its thick grass, its clear water, and
the protection from winter weather afforded by the
mountains on every side. Already, the foothills were
smeared with red and orange where the cottonwoods and beeches were turning color. The pines
higher up were dark green. In some places they
were almost black, and glistened in the sunlight.

They were heading north toward the San Andres
mountains, perfect country for letting horses run
wild. They could feed themselves, and grow strong
and healthy with a minimum of labor. Cougars
took a few, and Apaches occasionally skimmed a
few more, but it was still the most profitable way
to run a small herd.

The ground sloped uphill steadily, and by nine
o'clock, they could look back on the lush valley and

see clear across to the Childress spread on the far side of Las Cruces. Flashes of sunlight from half a dozen creeks seemed to slash like swords against the deep green of the valley floor.

"We penned the stock in a small box canyon," Sarah said. "We can use it for the rest of the stock. There are wild herds, too, and we can pick up a few head from one of them—if we get lucky."

"Whatever it takes," Slocum said. They were entering a cut with steep, rocky walls on either side of them towering overhead. Slocum looked up at the walls above him.

It was a good spot for an ambush, and the thought made him uncomfortable. Anyone traveling through the cut would be a sitting duck for a rifleman on the rim. Maybe, he thought, it won't come to that. He thought about saying something to Sarah, but decided that she had enough things to worry about.

Once they cleared the cut, Slocum found himself looking down into a shallow valley. The floor was bisected by a meandering creek, its waters occasionally white where they tumbled over boulders. The grass was lush and dark green. Across the valley, on the far side of the creek, was the reason Sarah had led him here—nearly three dozen horses were grazing in clusters of three or four. They were chewing lazily, and every now and then they looked up or paused just long enough to sniff the air.

"Time to go to work," Slocum said. "How many did you say Jason had penned?"

"Around two dozen. I'm not sure of the exact number."

"If we get all of these, we'll have just about enough."

Sarah gave him a tight smile. "That's the easy part," she said. "Getting them to Fort Stanton is going to be a lot harder."

"We'll manage. Don't worry about it. Let's see what we can do with these animals." He led the way down the slope, taking it at an easy pace, not wanting to spook the grazing horses. He checked either end of the valley, and saw that one end funneled through rock chimneys and seemed to lead to another valley beyond, while the other swept away and down in a long, slow descent to an even broader valley no less thickly grassed.

Slocum headed for the open end of the valley. He got beyond the last group of four horses, then herded them toward the far end, consolidating the smaller groups into one herd of twenty-five or thirty head.

He sent Sarah in a long loop toward the opposite end to block the outlet through the chimneys. The horses kept a wary eye on her as she rode past, but made no move to bolt. When she was in position, Slocum urged his mount forward, and the nearest of the horses looked up. It was a red stallion, and it pawed the ground and snorted once or twice before shaking its mane and turning to move off at a slow walk.

Slocum pushed ahead, and the stallion headed for the next cluster of grazers. They started to go even before he reached them, and now eight horses were on the move. They were starting to get nervous, but so far resisted the impulse to run flat-out. Slocum wanted to keep them as tranquil as possible, so he backed off a bit, knowing that they were close to stampeding.

He could see Sarah at the far end of the valley, and he waved to her. She waved back, then cupped her hands to her mouth, but whatever she shouted was whipped away by the stiff breeze blowing out of the cut.

It was apparent that the red stallion was the leader of the herd, and the key to controlling it was to keep him on a tight rein. The rest of the animals were alert now, and were no longer interested in grazing. They milled in tight circles; now and then one started off at a fast trot, only to stop and turn back the way it had come.

Slocum concentrated his attention on the red stallion now, and as he drove it past one group of horses after another, the size of the herd grew, almost as if by magnetic attraction. He was approaching the far end of the valley, and he saw Sarah, her body taut as a bow, watching the approaching herd as if expecting something to go wrong.

It took more than an hour to get the herd into a tight configuration, but that was the easy part. Now they had to get them to the canyon where the others were penned. Slocum did a quick count—there were thirty-seven. Added to the horses Jason and Sarah had already rounded up, they would be more than enough to meet the requirements of the contract. And there would be nearly a dozen left over.

He rode over to Sarah and stopped alongside her, watching the horses mill around nervously. "The big red stallion is the key," he said. "I think our best chance is to get a rope on him. If we can lead him, the others will follow. It'll be a hell of a lot easier than driving them."

Sarah nodded. "You're the expert, Mister Slocum. I wish I could do more to help."

Slocum shook his head. "I'm not sure it'll work, but it's worth a chance." He smiled. "Besides, there's plenty for both of us to do. You'll have to ride drag and make sure none of the skittish ones try to bolt."

"What if they do?"

"Just cut them off and make a little noise, they'll get back in line—in theory, anyhow. Where are the others?"

"About five miles from here. When we get back to that little creek, head upstream. The creek falls into the canyon and flows out through its mouth."

"We might have some problems if there's another feisty stallion in the bunch Jason rounded up."

"What'll we do then?"

"Let's cross our fingers and hope we don't have to find out."

He smiled, but she nodded gravely, her face was a mask of concern.

Starting to move away, he grabbed the rope from his pommel, and said, "Here goes nothing."

He moved around the edge of the herd to try and slip up on the red stallion, but the big horse was too wary for that. He kept snorting and moving away. The other horses followed him, and Slocum was forced to move in among them, keeping the rope ready, inching closer and closer. When he was finally close enough to give himself a reasonable shot at getting the rope on the red, he twirled it overhead, worked up enough momentum, and let it fly.

He jerked the reins on his gray, and it dug its heels in as Slocum pulled on the lariat even before the loop settled over the red's head. The big stallion, sensing something amiss, reared up, and Slocum hauled on the rope until he had a snug catch. The red bucked and reared trying to throw off the rope, and the other horses moved away, almost as if they were watching their leader to see whether he still deserved their trust.

Slocum looped the rope around his saddle horn, and slid from the saddle. He followed the rope, keeping one hand on it in case the stallion ran back on him. But the big red was too angry for anything so mischievous.

Slocum kept talking to the animal, keeping his voice firm, but reassuring. "Steady, boy, just hold on. I won't hurt you. Hold on, now."

The red, seeming to realize that he had no chance of tossing off the rope, finally calmed down, and Slocum moved in close enough to pat him on the flank. The horse was trembling, and kept tossing his head. He turned as if to bite his conqueror, and twice kicked with a vicious lash of his hind legs. Slocum snatched a fistful of the lush grass and got in close enough to offer it to the red, who turned up his nose, shook his mane, and whinnied with what sounded like annoyance. But he took the grass, and soon Slocum was able to rub his muzzle. Now their work really began.

8

The horses were corralled, and Slocum was exhausted. The next day would be even more tiring; they still needed to brand the animals in preparation for the drive to Fort Stanton. He needed a meal, and he needed a bath and a shave, but most of all, he needed to sleep.

As he walked around the corral to check the fence, Sarah Bridge stepped onto the porch and watched him. He was aware of her presence, but said nothing. He was drawn to her, which didn't surprise him because she was an attractive woman. But she seemed to be attracted to him, too, and he wondered whether it was genuine or his imagination. Or maybe, he thought, it was just indebtedness. He didn't want to misread her and do something that he would regret, and that she would resent.

When he finished walking the perimeter of the corral, he started toward the barn, and Sarah stepped off the porch and called to him.

"Mister Slocum, supper's ready."

He waved to her. "I'll be right there," he said, "I just want to get my horse fed."

She smiled and went back inside, leaving him to tend to the big gray. Removing the tack, he turned the horse loose in the small corral for ranch stock, carried the tack inside, and lit the lantern by his makeshift bed. Standing with his hands on his hips, he looked around the barn. At his age, he wondered how he had managed to live so long and have so little to show for it. He heard footsteps behind him, and turned with his hand moving toward the Colt on his hip, but it was just Sarah.

"What were you thinking about?" she asked.

"Nothing."

"Oh, yes you were. What was it?"

"Nothing, really," he repeated, more sharply than he'd meant. To soften it, he added, "I was just, you know, taking stock I guess you might say."

"Taking stock of what?"

"My life."

"Oh. Is it that bad?"

Slocum grinned, "I suppose not. It's just that a man gets to be my age, he kind of naturally wants to look back, see where he's been, maybe get some idea where he's heading."

"And you didn't like what you saw, did you?"

"Nothing much to like. So—no, I didn't much like it, but you have to put the best face on things."

She moved closer to him, folding her arms as if to hug herself. She stopped when he looked at her sharply. "Don't you have any family?" she asked.

Slocum smiled. "Family? Not hardly. I've been drifting for so damn long, I . . ."

"I'm sorry, I shouldn't pry, but you seem so . . . sad, I guess is the only word for it, and. . . ." She shrugged.

"You get used to it after a while."

"Still, family means a lot. It helps when there's someone you can lean on, somebody you can turn to when you need to."

"My life has been spent learning how not to need anybody," Slocum said. "There are times when you can't lean on anybody but yourself, when you can't trust anybody to know what you feel or what you need."

"And what is it that you need, exactly, Mister Slocum?"

"That," Slocum said, "is the real mystery, isn't it? Do any of us ever know the right answer to that question? I sure as hell don't."

"There's no law that says you have to drift forever. You could settle down anytime you want to, you know. Maybe you should think about that. Maybe you should *do* it." She stepped closer to him, reached out, and rested a hand on his arm. "You could, you know."

Slocum took a deep breath. "I don't think so. I'm too used to living this way. I think I'd get restless. If I settled down, soon enough I'd start to feel like I was in prison. You have no idea what that's like."

"I gather that you do?"

Slocum nodded. "Yeah, I do."

"But it doesn't have to be like that. I would imagine that when you're in jail, you understand that you can't go where you want, when you want. That's what makes it punishment. But if you're not in jail, then you don't *have* to move just to prove that you *can* move. But that takes time, maybe even courage to learn."

"Are you suggesting that I settle down, Miss Bridge?" Slocum teased.

She blushed then, and relaxed a little. She squeezed his arm once, then let her hand fall away. "I guess I sound so earnest. . . ."

"No need to apologize. You're not asking me questions I haven't asked myself before—some of them a thousand times—and I don't know the answers. I don't know why I live like I do, except that it seems like the only way I know how to live. Maybe I'm scared of trying something different."

"I can't imagine you. . . ."

"What?"

It was her turn to grow quiet. Finally, she seemed to remember why she had come to the barn in the first place. "Supper's getting cold," she said. "We'd better go on in."

She walked out of the barn then, leaving him to stare after her. He took one more look around, and followed Sarah to the house. Inside, he was surprised to see Jason Bridge sitting at the table.

"How are you feeling?" Slocum asked.

"Like I've been shot at and hit," Jason answered. He smiled, but it took considerable effort. "I can't thank you enough for what you're doing for my sister and me, Mister Slocum."

"No need. I remember reading somewhere that the enemy of my enemy is my friend. That seems to make us friends, sure enough."

"It's not that simple," Jason said. "You're really sticking your neck out, and Ray Sadler is likely to lop off your head, if he gets the chance."

"I'll worry about that later," Slocum said. "Right now, we have to get your horses over to Fort Stanton. This business with Sadler will sort itself out."

Slocum took a seat at the dinner table, and watched Sarah as she piled each of three plates with boiled potatoes, then placed a platter covered by a pair of thick beefsteaks in the center of the table. Sitting down, Sarah brandished a large fork, stabbed one of the steaks, and placed it on Slocum's plate. She cut the second one in half, gave a piece to her brother, and took the remainder for herself.

A pitcher of water and a pot of coffee sat at one corner of the table and, after pouring herself a glass of water, she offered the choice to the two men. Slocum opted for coffee, but Jason took water. Slocum reached for a sharp knife to cut the steak, but Jason held up a hand, bowed his head, and said, "Lord, for these blessings, we thank you. And we thank you for the help of a friend in a time of need. Please look after us all. Amen."

Slocum thought about commenting on the prayer, then decided against it. Praying made him a little uncomfortable, at least in public, and he wondered what it was that enabled some people to trust in the Almighty for help, when it seemed to come to them so seldomly. But it wasn't his place to say anything to Jason Bridge, or anyone else, for that matter.

"One thing puzzles me, Mister Bridge," Slocum said, after taking a sip of coffee.

"What's that, Mister Slocum?"

"When the sheriff asked who shot you, you told him you didn't know. Why? Why didn't you tell him Ray Sadler had done it?"

It was Jason's turn to feel uncomfortable. He lowered his eyes for a moment, then looked directly at Slocum. He chewed on his lower lip for a second or two before answering. "Because Walt Kennedy already knew. Because Walt Kennedy won't do anything about it anyway. And finally, because as long as I don't say anything, then I pose less of a threat to Tom Childress, who is my real problem, not Ray Sadler."

"But you have to realize that Sadler will try again. He can't count on you keeping silent forever. Even if he could, there is still the matter of your land, which Childress seems to want, and he seems willing to do anything to get."

"What's your point, Mister Slocum?"

"My point is, you have to stop them anyway you can, and the sooner the better. The longer you wait, the more likely it becomes that they will succeed, to your sorrow and, perhaps, with the loss of your life as well as your land. Then there's your sister to think about. She's in danger, too, don't forget."

"Do you honestly believe I'm not aware of that, Mister Slocum?" Bridge raised his voice, and winced with the effort.

"I don't know what to believe, Jason," he answered, trying to calm the young man down.

"I don't know what else to do. The law here is useless—worse than useless. The people are all cowed into silence, terrified of Sadler and his bullies, and dependent on Childress for almost everything. That means I'm on my own. I have to do whatever I can to survive. I'm not about to take a rifle and go up against Sadler and Childress on my own, and I know that no one else will join me. That means swallowing a little pride, telling white lies, maybe even selling a little bit of my soul. I know all that. But—" he stabbed at the steak on his plate, sliced a piece off, and chewed it voraciously before finishing—"if you have any ideas, I'd be glad to listen."

"I have an idea," Sarah said. "I think we should eat before the food gets cold."

Slocum nodded his agreement, and Jason Bridge smiled. "Look, Mister Slocum," he said, "the main thing here is that we get those horses to Fort Stanton. In a few days, I'll be back on my feet, and we can talk about this then. Besides, I imagine by then you'll be ready to move on. It's our problem, and we'll have to handle it somehow—and we will."

Jason turned to his meal, and the conversation stayed away from the touchy subject of Tom Childress. Sarah cleared the table with Slocum's help, then brought out an apple pie, cut generous wedges for each of them, and poured coffee for herself and Jason after freshening Slocum's cup.

When dessert was behind them, Sarah said, "If you want a bath, Mister Slocum, I can show you where."

"Are you suggesting that I'm a little ripe, Miss Bridge?" Slocum asked, grinning.

She wrinkled her nose, reminding Slocum of a rabbit, and said, "To tell you the truth—"

Slocum held up a hand. "I'd rather you not answer that," he said with a laugh.

Jason said, "One thing about Sarah, she doesn't really understand how a man can work up a sweat and not mind it. All that primping, powders and such that women go through—I never did get it."

Sarah defended herself immediately. "One day you'll understand. Some pretty young thing will catch your eye, and you'll be dousing yourself in stink water that'll draw bees from three counties. Talk to me about it then."

Jason laughed, winking at Slocum. "I just happen to have a bottle of stink water, as you call it. Perhaps Mister Slocum will want to borrow some. Seems like he's caught somebody's eye himself."

Sarah blushed again, and this time got up from the table and hid her embarrassment in a flurry of activity with the dishes. Jason got to his feet and limped over to stand beside her. "You go on ahead and show Mister Slocum. I'll tend to this business."

"It's all right, I—"

"Go on, Sarah," Jason said.

She nodded, went into another room, and came back with a stack of towels and a bar of brown soap. Leading Slocum outside, she said, "Don't pay any attention to Jason. He likes to tease, is all. I wouldn't want you to think I. . . ."

When she stopped, Slocum asked, "What is it you wouldn't want me to think, Miss Bridge?"

"Nothing," she said.

She moved ahead of him, heading for a stand of willows beyond the barn. Moving into the trees, she held the branches aside for Slocum, then pointed to a deep pool in a creek. "It's a lot easier than lugging buckets of water to the house, except in cold weather," she said. Then, as an afterthought, she added, "Do you have a change of clothes? Because I can wash these for you."

Slocum nodded. "In my saddlebags."

"Bring the wash up when you're finished," she said. "Do you need anything else?"

He shook his head.

"All right. I'll let you be, then."

She brushed back through the willow branches and was gone. Slocum wasted no time stripping down and wading out into the pool. The water was cold, but it felt good. It soothed his tired muscles and drained some of his exhaustion. The water was deep enough so that he couldn't feel the bottom until he was close to either of the banks.

Climbing half out of the water, he snatched at the soap, and lathered himself all over, working his hair into a mass of suds, then ducking under to rinse away a few days of sweat and trail dust. Then, lying on his back in the water, he closed his eyes, floated close to the bank and let the water recharge him.

He was half asleep and drifting off, concentrating only on the water lapping against his ribs, and the electric tingle of the current gliding past his skin, when he heard something and jerked his head up, shaking it to get the water out of his ears.

It was Sarah. She stood there with a shirt and jeans pressed against her bosom. "Sorry to disturb you," she said, "I just, well, I thought I'd bring your clean clothes down and take the wash now."

He nodded, forgetting for a moment that he was naked, until he saw her eyes lingering on his body, and a slight hint of red in her cheeks. He ducked down into the water then, and Sarah set the clean clothes down beside the towels, took the clothes to be washed, and straightened up again. "Sorry for bothering you," she said.

A moment later she was gone.

9

Jason and Slocum played poker for toothpicks while Sarah sat on an overstuffed settee, reading with a book in her lap, and a frown on her face. After Jason had cleaned him out for the second time, Slocum gathered the cards and said, "I think I'd better get some shut-eye before I end up owing you a box of toothpicks."

Jason laughed. "Cards was the one thing I was always lucky at. Don't ask me why, because I haven't the faintest idea."

Sarah looked up from her book to say, "Oh, yes you do. Daddy taught you."

"She is obliquely referring to the fact that our father made his living as a gambler from time to time."

"Try *all* the time," Sarah said, "when he was sober enough to remember what cards he had. The rest of the time, he supported other gamblers by hocking the family silver."

"It wasn't that bad, Sarah," Jason said. "Besides,

Mister Slocum doesn't want to hear about our father's weaknesses."

"No, I suppose he doesn't."

Slocum got up from the table, stretched, and said, "I guess we'd better get working at first light, Miss Bridge. It'll take all day to brand those horses."

"I might be well enough to give you a hand," Jason offered.

"I don't think you'd better push yourself, Jason," Slocum said. "The longer you rest, the sooner you'll be well enough to get back to work full time."

Sarah closed the book, making sure to put a bookmark at her place, and set it down on the end of the settee. Getting to her feet, she said, "I'll walk you out."

"No need," Slocum said.

"That's all right. I want some fresh air, anyway. The fire always makes me feel stuffy."

"Good night, Jason," Slocum said.

"Night, Slocum, and thanks again for everything you're doing for us."

"Don't mention it."

He walked to the door and held it for Sarah, then stepped out into the cool air. "Nice night," he said, as he stepped off the porch.

"I love this time of year. It gets chilly at night, but I don't mind."

Slocum walked toward the barn. Its door was yawning wide, and from it spilled an orange oblong of light onto the packed earth. Sarah followed right behind him. "You have enough blankets, Mister Slocum? It can get rather cold."

"I'm used to it, Miss Bridge. I'll be fine."

He went into the barn, turned to say good night,

and realized she was still following hard on his heels. She walked past him and sat down on a pile of hay. "I want to apologize," she said, "about before. . . ."

Slocum was puzzled. "I don't know what you mean," he said.

"Before, when you were bathing. I didn't mean. . . ."

"No apology necessary. It was kind of you to take care of the clothes that way."

"I should have had more respect for your privacy. I mean, there you were. . . ."

"In my birthday suit?" he laughed. "Let me tell you something, Miss Bridge, a man never minds having a visit from a beautiful woman, whether he's wearing clothes or not. In fact—"

"I know what you're going to say. Don't."

He thought she might be offended, but she was smiling, and he laughed.

"After all," she said, "it's not like I don't know what a man looks like. But. . . ."

"Well, at least you know what I look like," he teased.

"Yes, I do, and I must say I've seen better." She laughed then, at last allowing herself to be at ease. "But I don't suppose I have reason to feel so smug. I'm not exactly a goddess, myself."

Slocum took a step closer. "I can only speak for myself, Miss Bridge, but I'd prefer a woman to a goddess any day of the week."

"And twice on Sunday, Mister Slocum?" she asked, sticking out her tongue.

"Well, it *is* the Lord's day, after all. What better day to do the Lord's work."

"Is that what it is?"

"It ought to be, Miss Bridge. It ought to be."

"You must think me terribly forward, Mister Slocum."

"Not at all. I like plain speaking. You're an attractive woman, but I believe I've already said as much."

"Yes, as a matter of fact, you did."

She took a step closer, and now they were within arm's length. She was trembling, and Slocum reached out to her, taking one of her hands in each of his. He started to pull her closer, but she stiffened. "I think I should go back to the house," she said.

"Is that what you want, Miss Bridge?"

"I don't know what I want, Mister Slocum." She walked quickly to the door where she stopped without turning to face him. "And it's Sarah," she said.

She was gone before he could respond. Shaking his head, Slocum took off his shirt and sat down on his makeshift bed. Pulling the lantern close, he blew out the flame, and lay there in the dark with the tang of kerosene and smoke whirling around him. His thoughts of Sarah Bridge hung in the air, so palpable he thought he could reach out and catch them, the way he might fireflies.

Pulling off his boots and jeans, he lay down, rolled into the blanket, and tried to sleep. But sleep wasn't easy to come by. He kept thinking Sarah was coming back, and several times he imagined he heard her, but the tantalizing sound was just the creak of the barn door, or the hoot of an owl.

He lay there for what seemed like an hour before he heard something that had to be a footstep. Sit-

ting up, he was about to call out to her when he
heard a whisper. It was a man's voice, and the
whispered answer told him the man wasn't alone.

Suddenly, the smell of kerosene was sharp again,
and he thought for a moment he might have
knocked the lantern over. But when he groped
for it in the dark, he found it upright, just as he'd
left it.

Something was wrong, and he reached for his
gun belt, strapped it on, and pulled on his boots.
Just as he was getting to his feet, he heard the rasp
of a match being struck, flame spurted somewhere
beyond the open door, and he saw two shadows on
the ground, dimly etched by the match.

Then the flame seemed to mushroom, and he
heard footsteps moving away, not running, but
hurrying. He ran to the door in time to see two
men disappear around the corner of the house. The
barn door to his right was a sheet of flame, and he
ran back inside to grab a blanket.

Beating at the burning door, he managed to
smother the fire before it got fairly started. Then,
he tossed the blanket onto the ground, and tiptoed
toward the house. At the corner around which the
men had vanished, he stopped to listen. The smell
of kerosene was strong as he peered through the
darkness.

Once more, he heard a match being struck, and
he ran along beside the house just as flames erupted
at the next corner and the men came racing back
toward him. Slocum ducked, planted himself, and
took the lead man waist high, knocking him to the
ground. The man shouted, and the second man
hopped over his companion, landing a roundhouse

in midair. The blow caught Slocum in the chest and knocked him backward a step just as the first man got to his feet.

The attackers started to run, but Slocum raced after them, tackling the larger of the two around the waist, and shoving him to the ground. Using his leverage, Slocum hurled the man to one side, then leaped on top of him, pinning the man to the ground with both knees.

"Slocum!" someone called, and he half turned to see who it was. Then, something slammed into his shoulder, and his arm went numb, dangling uselessly by his side.

The man beneath him was squirming to get up, and Slocum had his hands full with the man who was still on his feet. He turned to ward off a second slashing blow from what he now realized was a rifle, and grabbed at the stock, but the wood was too slippery for him, and the attacker jerked it free.

The man he straddled was almost free now, and was trying to crawl out from under Slocum's weight. An arm looped around his neck dragged him back, but the momentary shift of his attention was costly for Slocum.

Once again, the rifle slammed into his shoulder, knocking him to one side. He hit his head on the wall of the house, and felt his consciousness starting to slip away. A split second later, he heard the sound of a rifle being cocked, then a door slammed, and one of the men said something Slocum didn't understand.

A moment later, the night exploded. The thunder of a shotgun being discharged, followed by a yelp of pain, were the last sounds he heard for several seconds.

When his consciousness returned, someone was kneeling over him, slapping his face to try to bring him to. He felt cold water splashed into his face, and heard voices. It took him several moments to place them—Sarah and Jason.

"What happened?" he asked, trying to get up against the pressure of a slender hand.

"Someone knocked you unconscious," Sarah said. "Jason heard you struggling with someone, but by the time I got out here with the shotgun, they had you down. I hit one of them, I think. At least it sounded that way."

It was coming back to him now. "The fire!"

"It's out. Thank God you heard them, or we might have been burned alive."

"They tried to burn the barn, too, but I put that out before I caught them over by the house."

"Did you get a look at them?" Jason asked.

"No. It was too dark, and everything happened so fast." He tried to get up again, and this time Jason held him back. "Let me sit up," he said.

"Get a lantern, Sarah," Jason said. To Slocum he added, "You stay down there until we can get a look at you."

"I'm all right. I hit my head on the foundation of the house, that's all."

"Are you sure?"

"I'm sure." He got to his knees as Sarah returned with a lantern. He took it from her, turned the flame up, and held it high.

"What are you looking for?" Sarah asked.

"I don't know, anything that'll help us figure out

who they were," Slocum said.

"As if we don't already know. . . ."

"There," Slocum said, stabbing a finger toward the ground, "blood. Sarah hit one of them, at least." He pointed out several smears of blood on the grass beside the house, and when he held the lamp closer to the wall, several drops of blood glistened in the light with thin trails left behind where they had run down the wall a couple of inches. "It's something, anyhow. If Ray Sadler or any of his cronies are carrying around a little buckshot in one of their worthless hides, we'll have all the proof we need."

"Proof for whom? You don't seem to understand, Slocum, nobody gives a damn. We're on our own."

10

Slocum was up before dawn. It had been a restless night, and he'd tossed and turned so much that by four-thirty he gave up altogether on trying to sleep. He saddled his gray and rode away from the Bridge spread needing time to think. It seemed as if he might have bitten off a whole lot more than he could chew.

It was one thing to watch your back sitting at a bar, and another to have to worry about being burned alive in your sleep. He realized that Ray Sadler meant business, and didn't seem to care much how he got things done, as long as he got what he wanted. Slocum wanted to believe that Sadler was a loose cannon, and was putting a little more pressure on Jason Bridge than his boss would have wanted, but the more he learned about how things had been unfolding in Las Cruces, the harder it was to believe that.

In the hills above the small ranch, he surveyed the valley. There could be no question that it was God's country. Once the moon went down, the

mountains were beautiful in the predawn light.
And almost as far as he could see, the land belonged
to Tom Childress. Jason and Sarah were hanging on
by their fingernails. They had a beautiful place. It
was small, but they worked hard, and they deserved
to keep it, not just because it was theirs, but because
that was the way things were supposed to be. You
kept what was yours, and you did the best you
could with it.

Tom Childress already had more land than one
man could ever use, and he still wasn't satisfied.
He wanted it all: lock, stock, and barrel. Slocum
knew only too well that if he got the Bridge place,
Childress wouldn't stop there. Men like him never
had enough—they could never have enough. Nothing was good enough for them. They pushed and
shoved their way to the front of every line. They
had to have the biggest houses, the fastest horses,
and the most beautiful women. They wanted all the
money there was, and even that sometimes wasn't
enough. It was greed, plain and simple. Slocum
had seen it often enough. He didn't understand
greed, didn't understand how it could eat a man
whole, but he sure knew it when he saw it. And he
knew it had to be stopped dead in its tracks.

Watching the sun come up, he saw the valley
reflect the sun's fire, first turning a deep red, then
a brilliant orange. Before the sun turned yellow,
he started back. He could see the road leading to
the Bridge house, and when he was halfway down
the last hill, he saw a solitary figure on horseback
riding hard toward the house, and kicking up a
cloud of dust that looked like boiling gold as it
swirled off into the grass.

Not knowing who it could be, and galvanized by the events of the night before, Slocum kicked the big gray and started for the road, hoping to intersect the rider before he reached the house. He was in full gallop and closing fast, but the lone horseman must have seen him because he lashed at his mount with the reins, and clapped his legs against the heaving sides of the laboring horse.

Slocum hit the road a good four hundred yards ahead of the approaching rider, turned the gray and drew his Colt. Charging up the road away from the house, he peered into the slanting sunlight trying to make out features on the man's face, but all he could see was a gray blur.

It wasn't until the distance had been halved that he pulled up, turned his horse, and blocked the road, keeping his gun hand toward the solitary horseman.

It was another one hundred yards before he recognized the figure of Phil Rattigan. Fifty yards later, he shouted, "Phil, what's wrong?"

Rattigan skidded to a halt a few yards away, shook his head, and said, "Christ, man, you scared the bejabbers out of me. I saw you comin' down the hill, and thought I was too late."

"Too late for what?"

"To warn you, man, what else."

"Warn me about what? You're not making any sense. Take a deep breath and pull yourself together."

"Late last night, I heard some cowboys talkin' in my saloon. They were drunk, and they were loud, the way they get, you know, and at first I didn't pay them no mind. But the more they talked, the more I listened, and I knew I had to get out here to tell you."

"Tell me what, dammit!"

"It was some of Childress's boys. They were talking about burning Jason Bridge out. Said they were coming out to set the place on fire—burn it to the ground."

"You're too late, Phil, we already know about it."

"How, in Christ's name, could you know about it already? I only heard them talking past midnight. It's not yet six o'clock."

"They came last night, before midnight, as a matter of fact. And they damn near got away with it. Luckily, I was in the barn, and they got careless, or—"

Rattigan blew his breath out in a grand sigh. "Thank God for good luck," he said.

"Come on up to the house. I'll put on some coffee."

"Are you planning to help with those horses?"

Slocum nodded. "Yes, why?"

"Because I got the feeling you'll never make it to Fort Stanton."

"I'll make it, all right."

"You can't herd them all by yourself, and you can't watch your back, either. It's too much for one man."

"Sarah Bridge is coming along."

"Sarah Bridge is a fine young woman, but she's no match for the likes of Ray Sadler and Bobby Coleman. You know that."

Slocum tilted his head as if to say, We'll see about that. But Rattigan was adamant. "You can't do it alone, man."

"Looks like I'll have to, Phil."

"No you won't neither. I'm coming with you."

"You can't do that. You have your own business to tend to."

"I can trust Twigs for a couple of days. He could use the money, and I can't afford to sit by and watch this anymore. The next thing I know, Tom Childress'll decide he wants to be in the saloon business. Then what'll I do?"

"Let's go on to the house, Phil. We'll talk about it there. By the way, do you have any experience with horses?"

Rattigan laughed. "Oh sure, and I do that, Slocum me boy. Sometimes I ride a big fire breathing stallion up and down behind the bar. The only problem is all the horse shit I have to clean up."

"I take it you don't," Slocum said, smiling, as he wheeled the gray toward the lane leading to the house. "But you'll learn a few things this morning."

Rattigan fell in beside him. "Such as what?"

"We have to brand the horses before we take them to Fort Stanton. Technically, they're already army property."

"Jesus, all that damn squealing, and the stink of burning horsehair. I don't know if my stomach is up to it, Slocum."

"We'll find out, won't we?"

"If only I'd known what I was letting myself in for," the Irishman laughed. "I think maybe I'd let Childress have the bar and wish him good luck when I handed him the keys."

"You don't mean that, Phil."

Rattigan looked suddenly grim. "No, Mister Slocum, I don't. I surely don't."

Sarah was up by the time they reached the house. She heard the horses and came outside. "Mister Rattigan," she said, "what are you doing here?"

"I've enlisted in the cavalry, for a few days only. Don't ask me why though, because if I think about it, I might not have a good answer."

Sarah looked puzzled. "I don't . . ."

"What he means," Slocum said, "is that he's volunteered to give us a hand on the drive to Fort Stanton."

Her face lit up then. "That's wonderful." Stepping down off the porch, she walked to Rattigan's horse. "I don't know what to say, Mister Rattigan."

"How about, 'Would you care for a cup of coffee, Phil?' That would be about the best thing you could say."

Without skipping a beat, she batted her eyelashes and said, "Would you care for a cup of coffee, Phil?"

"No thank you," he said. "I've brought my own liquid refreshment." He patted his hip and slid from the saddle with more grace than Slocum would have expected from a man who professed to know nothing at all about horses.

Sarah shook her head, then turned to Slocum. "How about you, Mister Slocum? Coffee?"

He nodded, climbed down from the gray, and tied it off at a hitching post beside the porch. Rattigan brought his own mount to the post and when he'd tethered it, all three of them went inside.

Jason Bridge was sitting at the table, reading a sheaf of papers. Looking up, he acknowledged Slocum, then knit his brow when he recognized Rattigan. Sarah, sensing his question, explained,

"Mister Rattigan is helping out."

Jason smiled. "I'll owe you one, Phil," he said.

"Sometime you might stop by and spring for a drink for the house," he said.

Jason folded the papers and handed them to Sarah. "This is a copy of the contract," he said. "You'll need this when you reach Fort Stanton. And you might let Colonel Anderson know, if you can, what's been going on here. He's a decent man, and I'm sure he won't look too kindly on Childress and his high-handed tactics."

"High-handed, is it?" Rattigan snorted. "I think that's far too gentle a description for what that murdering bastard has been trying to do."

Sarah poured coffee for everyone, and Rattigan, despite his initial reluctance, drank his after adding a touch of Bushmill's from his flask. In ten minutes, they were back outside, ready to cut the horses one at a time, brand them, and turn them back into the corral.

Rattigan got the fire going, Jason stood by to tend it, resting on a chair to conserve his energy, while Slocum and Sarah handled the animals and Rattigan used the iron.

It was sweaty work, and the horses were none too cooperative, but by noon they'd branded more than twenty. During a break for lunch, Jason said, "I think maybe we'd better be on the safe side, and send a few extra. We can always bring them back, or leave them at Stanton on account. I don't want to lose this contract if we show up with only forty-nine horses."

"What do you mean *we*, Jason? You're not going with us," Sarah said.

"I'll be there in spirit, at least." He smiled. "I wish we had another couple of days. I'd be well enough to make the trip by then."

"I don't think so," his sister argued.

"Well, it hardly matters. I can't do it now, and we only have until Friday. That's four days. A hundred miles is a long way to travel in four days."

"We'll manage it," Slocum said.

Jason nodded. "I know you will. But I can't help worrying. A man willing to set fire to a man's house isn't above much. And the three of you will have your hands full on the ride. I just hope. . . ." He let his words tail off, as if expressing his hope would be to liberate his deepest concerns—concerns better left bottled up for fear their liberation would give them life.

"We'll be fine, Jason," Rattigan said.

Slocum said nothing.

He wasn't quite so sure.

11

The road to Fort Stanton wriggled like a snake through rough terrain. The one hundred miles between Las Cruces and the fort wound through stretches of mountains, followed the Rio Grande river valley for nearly fifty miles, and then headed into the foothills of the San Andres Mountains. In some places, the road was little more than high desert. Slocum was worried most about the mountain stretches. Putting himself in Ray Sadler's shoes, he tried to decide where the best chances for a successful ambush might lie.

The first half of the trip was going to be the most dangerous. Since most bullies are looking for the easy way, it made sense to think that Sadler would try to strike early, keeping his own travel to a minimum, and staying fairly close to friendly reinforcements. The longer he waited, the further from help Sadler would be. Coupled with the reality of the country, and the probability that he would take advantage of high ground, the stretch through the mountains was the most likely place for Sadler to make his move.

Slocum traced the best route on a copy of an army map that Jason Bridge had marked in carpenter's pencil. "You're a lot more familiar with this country than I am," he said. "Show me the best places to get the jump on somebody driving a herd of horses."

Jason sucked on the end of the pencil, humming to himself. "If I was in Ray Sadler's shoes, I'd try one of three places," he said. Taking the pencil from his mouth, he followed the route with a fingertip, then marked a thick-armed **X**. "This is Coyote Springs. It's in a canyon nearly a mile long. There's high walls on both sides, and the canyon is narrow. Anyone up top can see anybody who goes through. And you have to go through it, because going around the mountains at this point adds a good twenty miles to the trip. Besides that, there's good water here. Anybody driving a herd is going to have to hit the springs here."

"All right, that's one," Slocum said. "Where's the next spot?"

"This one's closer to Las Cruces," Jason said, making a second **X** with the stubby pencil. "Apache Rocks. There's a five-mile stretch of the road that winds through some high buttes. They're not large, not like some of those further on, but there's a lot of them, and the road winds through a maze here. In fact, it's not really a road, because everybody going through picks the best route by instinct. All the valleys are narrow, and they connect like a fishnet or something. You can get through about fifty different ways. That sounds like you're on pretty safe ground, but the buttes give Sadler a real advantage. The approach is flat, and from up top you can see for miles. There are only three ways in and two ways out."

"Most likely, he'll have somebody watch to see us coming, then post his men somewhere inside where then can hit us before we can get to the exits," Slocum guessed.

"That's what I'd do," Jason agreed. "And the buttes are a sniper's paradise. A handful of Apaches up there held off nearly two hundred soldiers about three or four three years ago. The army couldn't get near 'em. They took about forty casualties, seventeen men killed, and the rest badly wounded. In the end, they were forced to try to starve the Apaches out, but they got away during the night. I don't think Sadler is that familiar with the Rocks, but you don't have to be to make them work for you. If he's got half a dozen men, he can cover three people easy. You'll be hampered by the herd, and all he's got to do is pick you off one at a time. Fish in a barrel."

"All right. Where's the third spot?"

Jason smiled. "Not that far outside of Las Cruces," he said. "All he's got to do is wait for you to pass through Johnson's Notch. You came through that with the herd when you brought it in."

"Yeah," Slocum said, "I remember. You don't have to tell me anything about it."

"Hell of a Sunday ride we're gonna take," Rattigan said.

"Last chance to jump ship, Phil," Slocum suggested.

Rattigan shook his head. "No, sir. I'm in for the long haul."

"You'll have to push them hard to make it in two days," Jason said. "I know we have three, but that'll give us a little leeway, in case there's any trouble."

"There won't be any trouble," Sarah said. "He wanted to stop us from rounding the horses up. Now that we've got them, he knows he's beaten."

Slocum shook his head. "I don't think so. I know his kind. He's probably mad that he hasn't stopped us already. That'll make him mean."

"Don't think you can frighten me into staying here, Mister Slocum. I'm going and that's final. You need me, and you know it."

Before Slocum could answer, there was a knock on the door.

"Who in hell could that be?" Rattigan asked.

Sarah walked to the door and opened it. Walter Kennedy stood on the porch. Behind him, still on horseback, Slocum could see two more men. He didn't recognize either of them.

"Morning, Miss Bridge," the sheriff said.

"What do you want?" she asked, not bothering to disguise her contempt.

"Got a complaint about you and your brother," he said.

"Complaint," Jason said, getting to his feet, "what kind of complaint?" He walked to the door and stepped out onto the porch with Rattigan right behind him. Slocum stayed inside, but kept an eye on the two men on horseback.

"Seems like somebody thinks you might have a few horses that don't belong to you, Jason."

"Oh?"

"That's right, and I couldn't help but notice as I

rode up that you had a pretty fair herd in the big corral over yonder." He cocked his head toward the army mounts, then smiled at Jason. "I expect those are the ones he means."

"You accusing me of horse stealing, Sheriff?" Jason demanded. "Because I resent it, if you are."

"Now, did I say anything about horse stealing, Jason? All I said was that somebody thinks you might have some of his stock. Maybe it was an accident, maybe it was on purpose. I don't presume to know which, and I reckon it don't make much difference, long as you give 'em back."

"Those horses are already sold, Sheriff. They are U.S. Army property."

Kennedy nodded. "I see. You tellin' me then, that all those animals were yours, is that it?"

"That's right. That's exactly what I'm telling you. Now if there's nothing further I can do for you, I have business to attend to."

"Well, I'm not saying you can do anything for me, exactly. But I got to take a look at them horses, see whether maybe there's some substance to the complaint."

"And I suppose the one who complained is Tom Childress?"

"As a matter of fact . . . yes, he is. How did you guess? I hope that don't mean what it just might mean."

"And what is that?"

"That maybe some of them horses in fact belong to Mister Childress. You mind if we take a look?"

"Look away, Sheriff. But make it quick. Those horses are leaving here in twenty minutes."

"That a fact? Well, I'd sure hate to inconvenience you, Jason. So we'll just wander on out to the corral and see what we can see." He turned to the two men on horseback, and said, "Come on, boys, let's go have us a look."

He climbed into the saddle, and nudged his mount in a tight circle heading toward the large corral where the army stock was grazing. Slocum came out of the house, and Kennedy looked at him sharply for a moment, almost as if he was surprised to see him. Then he smiled. "Pleased to see you done like I said and stayed around, Slocum," he said.

"You didn't leave me a lot of choice, Sheriff," Slocum answered. He climbed onto the gray, and fell in behind Kennedy and the two men, who he took to be Childress's hands.

"You hear anything about a shooting, Sheriff?" Slocum asked.

Kennedy shook his head. "Not since Jason got hisself shot I ain't—why? There been a shooting?"

"Somebody tried to burn the Bridges out night before last."

"That right?"

Slocum nodded. "Yes, that's right."

"And you shoot somebody, did you?"

"Not me, no. But one of the arsonists took away some buckshot he hadn't brought with him."

"Buckshot? No, ain't heard a thing about nothing like that. I suppose you could ask Doc Abernathy."

"I kind of thought it was more in your line of work, Sheriff," Slocum said.

"Well, it would be, I suppose, if anybody told me about it. I ain't had no complaints. Course, I didn't hear nothing about the fire, neither, so . . . looks almost kind of like folks don't want to overwork me, don't it?"

They had reached the large corral's fence, and Kennedy directed one of his companions to climb down and open it. When the rails were removed, Kennedy rode on through with Slocum right on his tail, and the two men followed, the one on foot replaced the fence rails before he remounted.

"Nice looking horses," Kennedy said. "Boys, you go ahead and take a look-see. You spot anything, let me know."

"What exactly are they supposed to spot, Sheriff?"

Kennedy shrugged. "How do I know? They ain't my horses. But could be they'll recognize some of the missing stock."

"Sheriff, you know as well as I do that none of those horses belong to Childress."

"I don't know any such a thing, Mister Slocum, and I ain't in a position to judge. Neither are you. We'll have to let the boys figure it out."

"Here's one of ours, Sheriff," one of the hands called out. "And here's two more." The cowhand pointed to a pinto stallion, and a pair of blacks that were almost identical with their hides shiny as coal in the morning light.

Kennedy looked at Slocum. "There," he said, "you see what I mean. Now I couldn't have done that, because they ain't my horses. But a man works with animals, he gets to know them like he knows his own kin. Hell, you're a cowboy, you know what I'm talking about."

Slocum ignored him and rode over to the hand

who'd identified the animals as belonging to Childress. "How do you know those are Broken C stock?" he asked.

"Recognize 'em," the hand answered. He smiled broadly. "See, we're missing a couple of blacks, and here they are."

"There's no brand other than the **US** brand, and I was here when that was put on," Slocum argued.

"Oh, hell, any fool can doctor a brand, Mister. I seen it done lots of times."

"There was no doctoring, I'm telling you. Those animals were unmarked when they were brought in."

"Them's our horses," the cowboy insisted.

"Here's a couple more," the other hand shouted.

Kennedy was shaking his head and clucking. "Unh, unh, unh, this sure is a fine mess," he said.

"They're lying Sheriff," Slocum said.

"Let's us go on back to the house. I think maybe I got to talk to Jason a minute."

Slocum started to object, but Kennedy ignored him and headed back toward the fence, this time jumping it rather than waiting for it to be opened. Slocum followed him, easing the big gray over the rails.

Kennedy pulled up in front of the house, where Jason and Phil Rattigan were waiting.

"Satisfied, Sheriff?" Jason asked.

"In a manner of speaking," Kennedy answered.

"Then you won't mind if we get on with our work. . . ."

"Well, I didn't say that. In fact, I got to impound those animals. Seems like Mister Childress was right. You got some of his horses in there."

"But that's a lie, and I have to get those horses to Fort Stanton."

Kennedy shook his head. "No, sir, those horses ain't goin' nowhere, until I get to the bottom of this."

The two hands pulled up alongside him, smirking. Jason lost his control for a moment. "You lying bastards!" he shouted. "You're—"

Kennedy raised a hand. "Hold on, Jason. It'll only take a few days to sort this all out."

"I don't have a few days, and Tom Childress knows it."

"Sorry, Jason. But that's the way it is."

12

Kennedy stood there with a broad smile on his face, watching Jason as if he'd just pulled off the perfect practical joke. Jason was nearly apoplectic, and one of the Childress hands made the mistake of goading him. "If you was smart, you'd have sold when the price was right, Bridge."

Jason took two halting steps, then, ignoring his bad leg and shoulder, he hurled himself through the air, catching the loudmouthed cowboy with his good shoulder, and driving him to the ground.

Jason straddled the man and closed his hands over his throat. "You son of a bitch, I'll kill you!"

The man began to struggle, but Jason was furious, and the harder the man resisted the more of his weight Jason drove through his stiffened arms. Kennedy was laughing, and the cowboy's partner was doubled over. "Shouldn'ta said nothing, Oscar," he gasped. "Might get you kilt."

The man on the ground was starting to gurgle, and his eyes had begun to bulge out of his head. Kennedy, realizing that things were on the verge of getting out of hand, said, "That's enough now, Jason. Let him up."

Bridge ignored him, and squeezed still harder. Slocum saw Jason's whitening knuckles, and realized that it was a no-lose situation for the Sheriff. He had the horses, and he had Jason, too.

"I told you to let him up, Jason," Kennedy barked, stepping closer and reaching for his pistol.

Slocum made his move then, and closed a hand over Kennedy's wrist. The sheriff jerked his arm free, but left his pistol holstered.

"I'll handle it," Slocum said.

"You do that," Kennedy snapped.

Moving alongside Jason, Slocum grabbed hold of his hands and pulled them from the man's throat. The cowboy lay there gasping with his neck a mass of bloodless white and angry red welts. "Come on, Jason, get up," Slocum said. "Get up. We'll figure some other way out of this mess."

Jason collapsed on his haunches, still straddling the hapless cowboy. He looked at Slocum with his eyes wide. A thick vein throbbed in his right temple, and his breath came in short gasps. Shaking his head, he mumbled, "It's over, Slocum. I'm finished." Then, burying his face in his hands, he began to sob.

"Grown man ought not to carry on so," Kennedy observed, and Slocum glared at him.

"You enjoy this, do you, Sheriff? You enjoy reducing a man to this? How the hell can you sleep at night?"

"I got no problems sleeping, Slocum. I sleep just fine, just like a baby." He tugged Jason Bridge off the still prostrate cowhand. "I'll be taking them horses now," he said.

"The hell you will!"

Kennedy froze with one hand still closed around Jason's arm. He turned to see who had spoken, but the look on his face suggested that he already knew.

Sarah stepped out of the house with a shotgun braced on one hip. "Just in case you're wondering, Sheriff," she said, "it's loaded."

Kennedy nodded. "Oh, I ain't wonderin', Miss Bridge. I know it's loaded. And I believe you would pull the trigger."

"You bet I would, Sheriff."

"This ain't gonna help matters none. You know that. You know I can come back with all the men I need, don't you?" He was turning his body slightly, and Slocum realized the sheriff was getting ready to go for the Colt on his hip. He moved in behind the sheriff and took the gun just as Kennedy tensed for the draw.

Backing away from the sheriff, he said, "Phil, disarm those two, will you?"

Rattigan quickly took the guns of the two hands, tucked them into his belt, and moved over toward Sarah. Taking the shotgun from her, he said, "Tend to Jason."

"You got to know this won't change nothing, Sarah," Kennedy said. "You won't get away with this."

She walked toward Kennedy, planted herself directly in front of him, and put her hands on her hips. "You're wrong, Sheriff. We'll get away with it, all right. And everything's changed now."

Kennedy laughed. "You're breaking the law to keep this place, but once you leave, you can't come back. Unless you want to spend some time in jail."

"I'll worry about that later, Sheriff," she said. "Right now, all I care about is delivering those horses—*our* horses. Once that's done, then we'll see what happens."

"Oh, you'll see, all right. You'll see what happens when you buck the law. You'll see what happens when you cross a man like Tom Childress."

"I already know, Sheriff. He's tried to kill my brother. He's tried to burn my home. He's tried to destroy us, and take everything we worked so hard to build. But he's not going to get away with it. And you can tell him I said so, the next time you get your paycheck."

"I don't—"

"Shut up! You're a pathetic little worm; a spineless creature who doesn't have the courage to enforce the law he's sworn to uphold. I don't give a damn about you and your threats, Sheriff. And I'll see you in hell, and Tom Childress right beside you, before I let him take away this ranch."

She turned away from him then, and went to Jason, who was starting to straighten up. He rubbed the tears from his cheeks and took a deep breath before trying to get to his feet. The attack had drained him, and he was forced to lean on Sarah as he hauled himself erect.

Slocum walked to Kennedy's horse, grabbed a rope from the saddle horn, and walked back.

"What are you gonna do?" Kennedy asked, his eyes widening. "You're not gonna . . . ?"

"Hang you?" Slocum finished. "No. Even if it is no more than you deserve." He jerked Kennedy's arms behind his back, tied his hands securely, then used a buck knife to cut off enough rope for the other two. He tied each of the cowhands the same way, then ordered the three captives to walk to the barn.

Kennedy kept looking over his shoulder, trying to figure out what Slocum had in mind. Once they were inside, he ordered them to sit against the wall, then tied their feet in quick succession. Once they were secure, he walked back outside. "Phil, give Jason the shotgun," he said.

Rattigan handed the Springfield carbine to Bridge, who looked at the gun, then at Slocum.

"You're in no shape for the ride, Jason," he explained. "And somebody has to stay here to make sure we have enough time to get away."

Jason nodded. "Don't worry, they won't breathe unless I say so."

"Don't turn them loose unless you have to. But if anybody comes for them, don't resist. Once we're on the trail, we'll be all right. Just don't give anybody an excuse to shoot you."

"Nobody needed an excuse before," Jason pointed out.

Slocum nodded. "I know that. Keep a horse ready, and if you see somebody coming, no matter who it is, you hightail it. Once you're in the hills, they'll forget about you. For the time being, it's the horses they want. I wish we could take the prisoners with us, but we're shorthanded as it is, and we'll have our hands full."

"I'll be all right."

"Phil, you and Sarah put their horses in the barn. No point in calling attention needlessly."

Rattigan untethered the animals, grabbed two by the reins, and Sarah took the third. Slocum and Jason walked to the barn, and were already inside when the others entered.

Kennedy was squirming and trying to loosen the ropes, but he was having no luck. He glared at Slocum. "You know," he said, "you're the one I want. Without you, things never would have come to this, Slocum. And I promise you that I will make you pay."

"Sheriff, if you were doing your job, things never would have gotten out of hand. But you let Childress buy you. You probably thought doing a favor once in a while was no big thing, that a little extra money wouldn't hurt, and nobody would be the wiser. But once you sold him the first piece of your soul, he had a mortgage on it all."

"Don't preach to me, Slocum. You're in no position to pass judgment on anybody."

"Neither are you, Sheriff, neither are you."

"You better not come back, I'm warning you."

"Sheriff, if I worried about that, I'd put a bullet in you right now. But I'm not worried because you're a coward. You don't have the nerve to stand up to a man with a checkbook in his hand. I figure that means you'll have even less stomach for facing a Colt."

Kennedy spat angrily, but it fell short, and Slocum shook his head. "You can't even do that right," he said. "It would be funny if it weren't so pathetic."

"You bastard!"

Jason sat across the barn, balancing the shotgun on his bent knees. Kennedy, realizing he couldn't intimidate Slocum, turned his attention to the rancher. "You better not fall asleep, Bridge," he said.

"I'm not tired, Sheriff, don't worry about it."

"It's you'd better worry. When I get loose—and I will—you will be in the deepest shit you can imagine."

"Sheriff," Jason said, giving him a broad smile, "I'll tell you what . . . if I feel like I'm gonna fall asleep, I'll shoot the three of you first. That way I can get all the rest I need. How's that? Course, if you don't want that to happen, you can watch me real close, and if you see me nod a little, or my eyes close kind of heavy, then maybe you and your lackeys can kick up a fuss, just in case."

"All right," Slocum announced, "I think maybe we better get going. There's a chance Childress might send somebody out here to see what happened to his toy sheriff. The sooner we hit the trail, the safer we'll be."

"Be careful, Jason," Sarah said. She walked over and leaned down to kiss her brother on the forehead.

"You too, sis," he said. "Don't worry about me, I'll be all right."

Slocum led the unlikely trio out of the barn. He patted the map in his shirt pocket, then walked to his horse. Swinging up into the saddle, he said, "I hope you all have some extra ammunition in case things get hotter than we expect."

Rattigan nodded, rapped his saddlebags smartly, and said, "I kind of figured I might be in a bit of a war, so I came all prepared."

He mounted up, and the two men waited for Sarah. She seemed to be debating whether or not to go ahead with the plan.

"Anything wrong, Miss Bridge?" Slocum asked.

She shook her head. "No, not really. I just. . . ."

"You're wondering whether this is a good idea, aren't you?"

Sarah looked at him then. "No. I know it's not a good idea, I was just wondering whether there was any other way. . . ."

"There's not," Slocum said. "Not now. Not with the Sheriff tied up in your barn, there isn't."

"That's what I thought."

She climbed into the saddle and nudged her horse into motion. "We might as well get going," she said.

13

The best route to Fort Stanton followed the valley of the Rio Grande to the fork of Sierra Blanca Creek, then it headed west, parallel to the Sierra Blanca, but there were mountains everywhere, and there was no easy way to go. The possibility that Ray Sadler and his men might be out there somewhere tempted Slocum to think about striking out due west, and staying away from the river, but it was too much of a risk. Most of the land to the west was Apache country. Water was not that easy to come by away from the river, and Slocum didn't know the terrain well enough to risk it. One man on horseback could always find enough to drink, but a herd of fifty animals needed much more water, and that meant taking the river route. That reality, he knew, would not be lost on Ray Sadler.

They were heading up into the hill country, with Las Cruces behind them, and the San Andres mountains dead ahead. The herd kicked up a cloud of dust that a blind man could see at ten miles. That meant, as Slocum understood only too well, that Apaches could see it, and so could Sadler. He kept trying to tell himself that he was worried about nothing; that Childress was beaten, and that he would chalk the defeat up to experience and try again some other time. But men like Childress weren't made that way. They didn't like to lose, never lost gracefully, and sure as hell didn't walk away. And until the horses cantered across the parade ground of Fort Stanton, Childress had a chance.

By ten o'clock, Las Cruces was a memory. A glance over his shoulder showed nothing but grass and rippling water stretching due south to the purple smear of the Mexican mountains. Slocum was riding point, with Sarah taking one wing or the other, and Phil Rattigan bringing up the rear. The horses had settled into a steady gait, and all Slocum had to do was keep his eyes open—and his fingers crossed.

He knew that Sadler could be out there any-where, and that a handful of men could move a lot more quickly than the herd. If Sadler *were* out there, it might be the impact of a bullet, or the crack of a rifle that would announce that fact.

Slocum used field glasses often, and swept the hills on either side every few hundred yards. He didn't really expect to see anything, and so far he hadn't. But he knew it was that one time you didn't look, the one time you told yourself there was nothing to see, the one time you decided to take the lazy man's way, that got you killed. And there was no doubt in his mind that if Sadler made a move, it would be a deadly one. Jason Bridge had been lucky, luckier than a man has a right to expect. But there was no more luck, not for Bridge, and not for Slocum. Childress was desperate, and Sadler was more than willing to do whatever it took. There would be no more waving papers, no more hiding behind the transparent veneer of a corrupt lawman; the next time was for keeps.

Johnson's Notch was two miles away. It was a sharp cut through the hills, and was nearly half a mile long. The river occupied half its width, and narrow bands of grass and brush studded with a few cottonwoods filled either margin. The rimrock on either side of the notch was nearly one hundred feet high, and one man sitting midway up with a rifle could see it all. Half a dozen could keep anything short of a cavalry regiment from getting through, and Slocum didn't have a regiment behind him. He had a bartender and a woman. If he were to calculate the odds he would fold his hand, so he tried not to think about it.

Scanning the notch through the glasses as they drew closer, he looked for anything: a glint of sunlight off a careless rifle, a puff of smoke from a thoughtless cigarette, a cloud of dust kicked up by horsemen in a hurry. But the longer he looked, the less he saw. The rimrock looked jagged and forbidding, but deserted.

When they were a mile away, he dropped back along the left wing, picked up Sarah and waved Rattigan forward. When the Irishman had joined them, Slocum said, "I think we better water the horses before cutting through the notch. If there's any trouble, we might have to drive them hard. I don't want them thinking about anything but moving when we start through."

Rattigan nodded. "You see anything through them glasses of yours?" he asked.

"Nothing yet. But that doesn't mean there's nothing there. Anyhow, if it was up to me, I don't think I'd make a move yet. I'd want to wait until we were further from Las Cruces."

"Apache Rocks?" Sarah asked.

"Yeah. It's about halfway, it's no-man's-land, and you could leave a hundred bodies out there with no one the wiser."

"You think they mean to kill us, then?" Sarah asked. It was a matter-of-fact question; there was no fear, and no womanly quivering of her lip. Slocum looked at her in surprise, as if he'd learned something important.

"It's what I'd do," he answered, using the same neutral tone. Then he added, "Of course, I believe we'll have something to say about it, assuming they find us, which is by no means certain."

Sarah took it well. She smiled, and reached out to grasp Slocum's forearm. "I guess we're depending on you then, Mister Slocum, aren't we?"

"I can't speak for you, Sarah," Rattigan said, "but I sure as hell am. I get out from behind a bar, and I get lost on the way to church."

"I didn't know you went to church, Mister Rattigan," Sarah said.

"See what I mean?"

He laughed, and Sarah shook her head. "I don't know why I even bothered to ask."

"All right," Slocum said, "let's get those horses to the river."

They were less than a half mile from the river,

and they dropped back behind the herd, arranged themselves in a broad vee, and drove the horses due west. Fifteen minutes later, the herd spread out along the riverbank.

The drovers dismounted to water their own horses, and Slocum took some jerked beef from his saddlebags and divided it. "I don't guess we'll be having much to eat before nightfall," he said, passing the small portions to Sarah and Rattigan.

"God above, I hate jerked beef," Rattigan said, tearing into a piece of the meat. "Salty as all get out. My stomach cries out for a thick steak every time I get within ten yards of this dreadful stuff. It just makes me crave real food."

Sarah ate hers without complaint, and in fifteen minutes they were ready to move out. Once they got the herd moving, Slocum said he wanted to go on ahead, just in case.

"It might not be a good idea to divide us," Rattigan suggested.

Slocum disagreed. "If Sadler's gonna make a move, he'll wait until we're all together. He can't take the chance one of us might get away."

Sarah said, "I can't believe how calmly you two are discussing this. You're talking about men who will kill us if they get the chance, murder us in cold blood, and you treat it like it was some kind of game."

"It's still not too late to turn back," Slocum said. "But if you think that will make a difference to Sadler and Childress, you're making a big mistake. The only way to get out of this is to beat them at their own game. We'll get these horses to Fort

Stanton, then go back to Las Cruces and confront them."

"I know," Sarah answered, "I know that, but. . . ."

"I'll be back as soon as I can." He didn't want to give Sarah any more time to think about things. It was best if they all just kept moving. He spurred the gray and headed away from the river, angling toward Johnson's Notch.

A quarter of a mile from the mouth of the tight canyon, he reined in, peered through the glasses, and examined the rim once more. Satisfied that it was deserted, he moved ahead, more cautiously now, with his Winchester cradled across his thighs. He approached at an angle, then moved along the sheer face of red rock toward the opening, where he dismounted.

Using what little cover the brush afforded, he sprinted toward some beech trees close to the river. The notch was only three hundred yards wide at its broadest point, and he wanted to cross it from side to side. If Sadler had beaten them there, there would be some sign in the sandy soil. Compressed by the notch, the river was too deep for horsemen to have entered it and ridden upstream, so there was a good chance he would see evidence of recent passage.

Working his way toward the river, he kept his eyes on the ground. He found some old prints, but they were from unshod hooves, more than a week old, he guessed, and probably Apaches. The thought made him wonder just what the odds of getting to Fort Stanton really were, but he pushed it aside quickly.

That left the far side of the river. Looking back

toward the herd, now three-quarters of a mile away, he saw the dust cloud it kicked up, and knew that there wasn't much time. He had to get across the river and check the other side. One hundred yards upstream, the river divided into several smaller streams where a series of sandbars blocked its passage, forcing it into several deep, swift channels.

Sprinting along the bank, he kept one eye on the rim to his right, until he came abreast of the sandbars, then he leaped across to the first of them. It was nearly ten yards across and solid. Leapfrogging, he made it two-thirds of the way across the one-hundred-yard width, but the last two sandbars were too far for him to jump. He had no idea how deep the river was, he couldn't see the bottom, and the water was moving so swiftly that it would knock his feet from under him in any case.

He could go back, but that would take too much time. The only choice was to swim. Moving to the upriver tip of the sandbar, he tossed both guns across the gap to the next bar, left his gun belt on the ground, and dove in. Pulling hard, he covered the thirty-odd feet just in time to dig his hands into the downriver end of the next sandbar, and scramble out of the water.

Retrieving his guns, he leapt to the last bar and onto the far bank. Working his way toward the opposite wall, he scrutinized the sandy ground, and found what he had hoped not to find—hoofprints, at least half a dozen sets, and recent. Instinctively, he looked up at the rimrock towering above him, but there was no sign he was being watched.

His worst fears confirmed, he looked upriver, knowing that Ray Sadler was ahead of him. Taking a deep breath, he whispered, "That tears it."

There was no choice now but to hold the horses downriver until he could check the notch. Retracing his path across the river, he retrieved his gun belt, and sprinted back to his horse. Sopping wet, he swung into the saddle and kicked the gray into a full gallop, heading toward the approaching cloud of dust.

Rattigan saw him coming, and rode out to meet him. "Trouble?" he asked.

Slocum nodded. "You bet there is," he said. Sarah had ridden over to hear the exchange. He looked at her before continuing. "There's a half dozen men ahead of us, at least. Recent tracks, and we have to assume its Sadler. We can't afford not to."

"What'll we do?" Sarah asked.

She sounded frightened, and Slocum sought to reassure her, but he was feeling anything but certain himself when he said, "I'll have to ride through the notch, see what I can find. I still think this is not their first choice. If the tracks continue on, I'll come back and get you. In the meantime, you'll have to wait here."

"What if the tracks don't continue?" Sarah demanded. "Then what?"

Slocum sighed. "We'll have two choices. We can fight it out here and now, or we can try to get through at night. There'll be some moonlight, but if we stay close to the wall, there should be enough shadow to give us some protection."

"I see," Sarah said.

"But let's hope it doesn't come to that."

"Yes, let's," Rattigan said.

14

Slocum left Rattigan and Sarah to handle the horses, and raced back toward the mouth of the notch. Three hundred yards before he reached the entrance, he nudged the gray into the river. The horse could walk part of the way, but suddenly the bottom dropped away, and the gray was forced to swim nearly fifty yards before the far bank rose up to meet his hooves.

Once across the river, Slocum pushed the animal at a full gallop until he reached the spot where he'd found the fresh tracks. He reined in, and debated whether to go ahead on foot, or to ride. It was Hobson's choice; if he ran into trouble, he'd need the horse, but on the ground he presented a less tempting target. Since speed was paramount, he stayed on the gray, easing ahead in twenty-yard increments, and always keeping one eye on the rimrock.

He'd gone about three hundred yards into the notch when he thought he saw something up high. He couldn't be sure, and as soon as he fixed his

gaze on the spot, whatever it was—if it was anything all—was gone. Easing the gray forward, he
kept his eyes glued to a cluster of boulders one
hundred yards ahead and close enough to the rim
that a man hiding behind them would have a clear
view into the notch in both directions.

He hated moving so slowly, but he had no choice.
Twenty yards further, he saw it again, a blur of
movement, something tan or dark beige, maybe a
man, maybe not. He'd seen too little, and had seen
it too briefly to be sure.

He leaned over to reach for the Winchester,
clicked off the safety, and levered a round into
the chamber. Bringing the rifle up, he sighted
on the rim to the left of where he'd last seen the
movement. He hoped he was wrong, but he was not
willing to bet his life that he was.

He held his breath, counting the seconds. *Ten . . .
eleven . . . twelve . . . thirteen . . . there!* There it was
again, a blur of movement rather than color. Then,
almost as if to make him feel foolish, a cougar peered
over the rimrock, looked right at him for a fleeting
instant, then disappeared.

Slocum exhaled slowly, and shook his head at the
bout of nerves, then nudged the gray on ahead. He
knew that the mountain lion on the rim reduced, if
not altogether eliminated, the chances that someone could be lying in wait. The animal would have
picked up a man's scent, and if he went to inves-
tigate, the sniper would have been forced to shoot.
You didn't just say, "Shooo!" to a cat that size.

He was almost halfway through now, and the
tracks were still there—steady, almost uniform,
as if the men had set a pace and were determined

to stick to it. He wanted to kick the gray into a full gallop and race through the notch, tempting fate and the uncertain marksmanship of Ray Sadler and his cronies, but patience was his only ally, and he struggled against the impulse.

The sun was high overhead now, shining almost straight down into the notch, and Slocum was starting to sweat heavily. Flies buzzed angrily from the brush and the tall grass as the gray moved through, and Slocum swept out an angry arm to keep them away. Conscious that time was slipping away, he pushed the horse harder into a canter now, relaxed a bit about the rim, and kept his eyes on the tracks ahead of him.

At the far end, the walls of the notch sloped down gradually, and with three hundred yards to go, they were less than seventy feet high, still high enough to give a commanding view of the floor, but less than perfect for an ambush. Kicking the gray once more, he urged it into a gallop, and chased the horseless tracks out into the next valley. Rather than waste time following them out into the open, he turned, and moved in toward the mouth of the notch and the river.

Once again, he forded the Rio Grande, and checked the ground one hundred yards or so past the opening, just to be sure the horsemen hadn't doubled back, then spurred the gray into a gallop back through the notch. At full speed, it took him less then ten minutes to reach the herd. Rattigan was lying in the grass and jumped up as Slocum approached. Sarah was sitting with her back against a cottonwood.

Slocum rode over to her, and without dismounting said, "All clear, from the look of things."

Sarah seemed to relax then, and flashed him the kind of smile he hadn't seen in a couple of days. "I guess we can go on through," she said.

"The sooner the better," Rattigan added.

"You might as well get in the saddle," Slocum said. "We have a long way to go before we can make camp. I want to be almost to Apache Rocks before we stop for the night. That gives us about seven hours, at the most."

Rattigan blew his breath out in a great stream, stood up, untethered his mount, and swung into the saddle. Sarah mounted her own horse with less exasperation and considerably more grace than the beefy saloon keeper. It took a few minutes to coax the horses into a tight knot, but within a quarter of an hour they were heading toward the notch.

"Just to be on the safe side," Slocum shouted, "I think we ought to take them through in a hurry. If for no other reason then because I spotted a catamount on the rim. If the horses get wind of it, they might spook. If we run them in, they'll keep on going."

Rattigan nodded. "Suits me. I don't much like them big cats myself."

"They're beautiful animals," Sarah said. "So fluid, so much grace."

"So many claws," Rattigan added, and Sarah laughed. It cut the tension for the three of them, and for a moment it was possible to forget about the perils ahead.

They worked the horses up to a full head of steam, and by the time the leader reached the

notch, the horses were going at a gallop. There
was some risk to the horses in taking the transit
so fast, but the risks were more than balanced
by the increased safety, and the time they would
make up.

The wall went by on the right in a blur of red
stone broken by slashes of gray and green where
the taller trees and brush reached up toward the
rim. There was enough room for Slocum to get on
the river wing and gradually work his way toward
the head of the herd.

Once he reached the point where the walls started
to slope, he moved toward the lead horse and turned
it, forcing the rest of the herd to follow suit. He
wanted to get away from the river a bit, and headed
east about one hundred yards. Rattigan and Sarah
slacked off, and with the insistent yips of the drovers now silenced, the horses began to slow.

A shallow depression, full of grass and watered by
a tiny creek, loomed up ahead, and Slocum headed
for it, leading the horses in, and slowing gradually
as he started downhill. It would be a good place to
regroup and let the animals calm down after the
excitement of the passage.

He walked the gray into the creek to let it drink,
and watched while the army stock milled in circles, some of the horses taking water while others
seemed content to pull at the lush grass.

After twenty minutes, he announced that it was
time to get moving again. "Let's try to set a steady
pace from now until nightfall," he said.

"Good idea," Rattigan answered. "I'm starting to
like the saddle again."

"What do you mean, again?" Slocum asked.

Rattigan grinned. "You don't think I stayed on the horse this long without a little experience behind me, do you?"

Slocum had been wondering about that very thing, but had chosen not to mention it. "What kind of experience?" he asked.

"There was a war a few years back. You might have heard of it?"

Slocum laughed. "Yeah, I heard of it."

"Well, I was a young lad, half my current size—or so it seems—and I thought it would be a grand thing to wear a uniform and fight for the Union." He looked at the sky and chewed on his lower lip before going on. "If only I had known then what I know now . . . I was wrong. It was not a glorious thing. Not at all. . . ."

"You don't have to tell me," Slocum said. "I was there."

"On the wrong side, too, I'll bet. I'll wager a bottle of Bushmill's on that," Rattigan said, laughing.

Slocum smiled, but said nothing.

"It's the accent, you see," Rattigan explained, now embarrassed. "I mean, you sound like a Johnny Reb, and I just naturally figured that you. . . ." He stopped in mid-sentence. "I guess you don't like to talk about it. Sorry."

"That was a long time ago," Slocum said. "A lifetime ago."

"I wish it was in another life altogether," Rattigan said. "It was . . . aw, hell, maybe I should just shut my gob."

Slocum nodded, hoping that Rattigan took no offense. The last thing they needed was to be squabbling over ancient history. All that would do is make them careless and sloppy. And out here, being sloppy could very well mean being dead.

"You got any more of that damned jerked beef, Slocum?" Rattigan asked, changing the subject abruptly and, Slocum sensed, permanently.

Reaching into his saddlebags, Slocum pulled out a hunk of the dried meat, tore off a piece, and tossed it to Rattigan. He offered some to Sarah, but she shook her head, so he tucked it back into the bag.

"Time to move," he said.

"None too soon, if you ask me," Rattigan said. "And I'm just as happy to chew this damned stuff as me own foot. I thank you, Mister Slocum. And I owe you a drink, your choice."

"Even bourbon and branch?" Slocum asked, smiling.

"Aye, even bourbon and branch."

"Then it's a dead issue, Phil." He spurred the gray and clucked to the herd. The horses moved reluctantly, but they moved. Once Sarah and Rattigan fell in behind the herd, Slocum moved on ahead.

He wanted to ride point until nightfall. As the most experienced of the three in open country, he felt it was safest for them all. Now they moved steadily down the center of a broad valley, with the river far to their left. The Rio Grande ran close to rocky hills in the west, and open country gave them the best chance to spot trouble before they rode into it.

He kept looking back over his shoulder, not wanting to get too much of a lead, but not wanting to lag, either. He hoped Sarah and Rattigan would find a pace that was neither laggard nor killing.

The stock was hardy but not invincible, and there was no point in delivering a bunch of played out horses the army would reject.

They stopped twice more for fifteen minutes each time, just long enough to give the horses a break, and the second time it dawned on Slocum that they were being more solicitous of the animals than they were of themselves. He was used to the saddle, but Sarah, despite her competence on a horse, was hardly a seasoned veteran, and Rattigan had spent nearly ten years behind a bar, or so he claimed. His head might remember the cavalry, but there were instincts and habits that would be slow to come back.

But neither of them complained. It had fallen to Slocum to lead, and they would follow, with their mouths shut and their jaws clenched. They would not utter a protest if it killed them to be silent.

Slocum was sensible of the hidden danger that might represent. If they were pushed beyond their limits, in an emergency they would be useless at best and maybe even a liability. But he didn't want to offend them, so he kept his own counsel, trying to gauge the toll the drive was taking on both of his companions. It was not beyond the realm of possibility that he would need their help with more than the horses, and he wanted to be able to count on them when the time came.

An hour before nightfall, they were bushed. Ahead, in the fading light, Slocum could see Apache Rocks, with its great mounds of red stone turned violet by the sheets of evening shade cascading over their sides. The last two miles saw the grass give way to mesquite and cactus, so he decided to camp for the night while there was still enough grass for the herd. They would tackle the approach in the morning.

15

As night fell, they drove the horses into a box canyon, then rigged a double line across the narrow mouth. It was easy enough, if you were determined, to drive off even broken stock, and the wild animals were even more skittish. A mountain lion would be enough to send all their work up in smoke, and with it went whatever chance Jason and Sarah Bridge had of keeping their ranch.

In the back of Slocum's mind was the very real possibility that Sadler and his men might have seen them already. If they were on the buttes at Apache Rocks, there was a better than even chance that they had seen the herd. Slipping in tight and running off the horses would only take a few pistol shots, a few yells, and then it would all be over. The Indians had been doing it for years, not only to one another but as a favorite prelude to an attack on the army. And if Sadler managed to get close enough to do it, there would be no chance to round up all the animals again in time to make the deadline at Fort Stanton, assuming he didn't kill the three of them before he was finished.

When the double rope line had been securely tied, Slocum said, "I think we'd better not have a fire."

Rattigan protested. "It'll get mighty cold tonight, John," he argued.

"I know, Phil, but we want every edge we can get. They might know where we are, but they might not. No sense sending up a beacon if we can avoid it. Besides, the fire might draw some other unwelcome company."

"Like who?"

"This is Indian country. The fire might draw a passing war party. We're cut pretty thin for Sadler and his boys as it is, against a handful of Apaches, we wouldn't have a chance."

"Never thought of that," Rattigan admitted, running a hand dramatically through his thinning hair. "Got little enough up top as it is. Wouldn't want to see the rest end up hanging in some wickiup."

"You don't really think we have to worry about Apaches, do you Mister Slocum?" Sarah asked.

Slocum shrugged. "I saw tracks in Johnson's Notch. Unshod ponies, which means Indians, and most likely Apaches. This is Mescalero territory, but even the Chiricahua come this far east on occasion. The tracks I saw were about a week old, maybe even older, so I don't expect it, no, but I don't want to do anything to increase the odds, either."

Sarah hugged herself, suppressed a shiver, and said, "All right, I guess we'll have to do without a fire."

"And," Slocum continued, "I think we should post a guard. Even without a fire, with the moon later tonight we still won't be that hard to spot, at least for anybody who has a good idea where to look. We'll have to take turns. I'll take the first watch."

"How long you want the shifts to be, John?" Rattigan asked.

"Two and a half hours, tops. That'll have us all running on five hours sleep. We have a full day tomorrow and, unless I'm wrong, our worst day."

"You expect Sadler and company to make a move at Apache Rocks?"

"You bet I do. Sarah, you'll take the second watch, all right?"

She nodded. "You'll wake me when it's time? I'll sleep like a log. I'm exhausted."

"You," Rattigan said, laughing. "I think a cougar could sit on my head and he'd think I was a rock. I know I sure as hell wouldn't know he was there."

Slocum smiled. "Don't worry, Sarah will find a way to wake you, I'm sure."

"When it comes time, what I'd suggest," Rattigan said, "is that you stick a bugle in my ear and blow it as loud as you can."

Sarah chuckled. "We don't have a bugle, Mister Rattigan, and I couldn't get a sound out of it if we did. I'll have to think of something else."

"As long as it's loud enough to wake the dead, it ought to work. At least the second time. Now, if you'll be so kind, John, as to pass out some of that shoe leather we've been eating, I think I'll have dinner and get some shut-eye."

Slocum tossed the saddlebags to Rattigan. "Help yourself. I'll be at the mouth of the canyon, on the right side, if you need me for anything. If you hear anything, anything at all, don't shoot and don't shout. Just come get me."

He got up, grabbed his Winchester and a box of shells, and walked into the gathering darkness. Near the canyon mouth, he found a small niche just inside the picket ropes big enough to accommodate him and to give him some cover, if he needed it. He settled down with his back propped up against a boulder. From here, he could see all the way across the mouth of the canyon.

The sky turned from charcoal to coal, and started to sparkle with stars. It would be at least two hours before the moon came up, and he figured it would be relatively quiet until then. Anybody wanting to move in on them would want to be able to see what he was doing. Sitting there, listening to the wind in the cottonwood leaves that were starting to turn color and to get brittle with autumn cold, he wondered how he had gotten himself into yet another tight squeeze.

"You have the knack, old son," he whispered, "you definitely have the knack."

He watched the sky, twice seeing a shooting star slash across the night, leaving a fiery trail in his eye long after it had winked out, and once, the shadow of an owl glided past. A moment later, he heard the frightened squeal of some unlucky rodent and the beating of great wings as the owl lifted off, dragging its prey skyward. He watched the sky for a bit, but the owl didn't come back his way, and soon it was quiet once more.

Behind him, an occasional nicker reminded him why he was sitting there as one or another of the horses grew momentarily restless. After a half hour, he had grown accustomed to the night sounds— the skitter of lizard feet on sand, the clink of a dislodged rock now and then as the canyon slowly but surely continued to change its shape, and the hiss of the wind in the trees. He was thankful for the chill settling over the terrain because it would keep rattlers, scorpions, and tarantulas at home. Laughing almost out loud, he considered the irony of sitting there not caring about creatures that walked with no legs, or with eight legs, and having to worry about the only creatures around that walked on two.

The war had taught him quite a bit about human nature, not much of it good, and the aftermath of the war had finished his education. Returning to a home that was no longer there, and a family that had vanished because of the worst excesses, he had taken his revenge and burned every bridge he'd crossed since.

At times, it seemed to him as if he were condemned, like some figure in an ancient poem that Homer had never gotten around to writing. He would crisscross the earth, never stepping on the same patch of sand a second time, as if he would never find a place that was truly his own; where he was welcome and could welcome others. He'd seen so many people try to carve a place for themselves, using picks, shovels, and fingernails, but there always seemed to be somebody who wanted to take it away from them. To have roots, it seemed, was to invite treachery, and he wondered who was better off—the man who tried, whether he failed or not, or the man who had sense enough not to try at all.

There was no answer to the conundrum, and he had long since realized that, but he kept on puzzling through it again and again and again, hoping that one day it would all make sense.

A stealthy footstep fractured his reverie, and he tensed, closing his hand around the Winchester, and curling his finger through the trigger guard.

Cocking his head toward the sound, he heard another footstep, then a third.

As he was about to get up, he heard a whisper, "John, John?"

It was Sarah, and he sighed with relief. "Over here," he whispered.

He stood up then, and her shadow suddenly materialized out of the darkness. "I brought you some blankets," she said. "It's too cold to be sitting here without something to keep off the chill."

She held them out and he took them with thanks. "I couldn't sleep," she said. "I'm frightened, and I don't know if I can do this. . . ."

"You'll do it," he said. "I won't let you not do it."

"I still don't understand why you should care," she said.

"I don't understand it either," he told her, realizing as he said it that it was true. She was shivering, and her arms were hugged to her chest. He took one of the blankets and draped it around her, then wrapped himself in the other and edged back into the niche. She squeezed in after him and sat down, drawing up her knees and covering them with the blanket.

Slocum sat beside her. "All you have to do is keep your mind on that one thing—Fort Stanton. We'll get you there, and we'll get you home. I don't expect that Childress will go away, but at least it will buy you some time."

She nodded. "I know. . . ." Her teeth were chattering, and Slocum rearranged his blanket to encompass her as well, and put an arm around her shoulder.

"That feels nice," she said. "It's as warm as I've been in a couple of hours. Maybe ever." She leaned her head back, and closed her eyes. "Maybe I'll just sleep here until it's time for my watch."

"Wouldn't you be more comfortable back by the horses? These stones are hard, and you'll have a few hours to put up with them."

She sat up then. "John Slocum, are you telling me you don't want me here?"

Slocum shook his head. "Not at all, Miss Bridge. I just—"

She placed an upright finger to his lips. "I told you before, call me Sarah." Then before he realized what was happening, she leaned forward and pressed her lips to his. It started as a peck, but she continued, and he felt her tongue against his lips. He opened his mouth, and her tongue slid inside like liquid fire. He responded, and let his hand rest on her stomach for a moment, until she reached down, closed her hand over his and guided him higher. The fullness of her breast filled his palm, and he rested his thumb on a stiffening nipple.

She broke away then, and he thought she was angry, but she smiled. It took him a moment to realize that she was unbuttoning her shirt. Then, with the primness and efficiency of a schoolteacher, she took his hand and brought it back. This time, her smooth, cool skin trembled under his hand.

"That's better," she said, leaning forward to kiss him again. He let his lips wander, tracing the curve of her lips, then the firm line of her jaw, and down to the hollow of her throat.

Despite the long day on the trail, she felt cool and smooth, and there was a hint of the scent of flowers on her skin. His lips closed over her nipple, and he opened his mouth wide to suck the heavy lushness of her breast. His tongue lapped at the pebbled aureole, and the stiff insistence of her nipple goaded him, then she moaned.

He felt her hands on his chest, then they fluttered like moths over his ribs until they rested in his lap. He was hard, and she felt it with the back of her hand. Rubbing without turning his hand over, she made him harder still. Then, turning her hand until her fingers could curl around him, she squeezed gently, stroking through the denim, and tracing the head with her fingertips.

He sucked at her breast a moment longer, then rested his face in the hollow of her stomach as she leaned back with his cheek pressed against the slickened skin. He felt her hands in his hair then, stroking softly, twirling ringlets in her fingers. "I wish. . . ."

When she stopped speaking, he lifted his head. "What?" he asked.

Shaking her head, she pulled her shirt closed, tucking it between his mouth and her breasts, then pressed his head back down. "I'm afraid I might be fooling myself, mistaking gratitude for something else."

"What?"

"Love . . . or lust."

He nodded. "I understand."

"No, I don't think you do. But I will, and when I do, maybe then. . . ."

"I'll be ready."

She dropped her hand to his lap, curled her fingers once more around his stiffened cock, and said, "You already are." She laughed then, girlishness tinged with bitterness. "I just don't know if I am."

She got up then, and he watched her slowly button her shirt as the moon climbed over the horizon. Its light seemed to paint her skin dark silver, and as she covered her breasts and pinched the buttons home one by one, he felt as lonely as he'd ever felt in his life.

16

Slocum studied the map, while Rattigan and Sarah leaned over his shoulder. "It looks to me like there's no easy way through Apache Rocks," he said.

"We're doing all right, so far," Rattigan reminded him. "No sense in throwing in the towel before anybody even throws a punch."

"I'm not throwing in the towel, but I think I have to ask ourselves a few hard questions before we walk right into an ambush."

"I'm all ears," Rattigan said. Then patting his ample belly, he added, "And a little stomach, too."

Slocum laughed in spite of himself. "If Ray Sadler would agree to die laughing, Phil, I reckon we could send you in alone, that would probably get it done. But since he won't, we better figure out what we want to do. Better to know than to have to improvise once the lead starts flying—which it surely will."

"You got any ideas, John?"

Slocum mumbled under his breath, tracing one route, then another, and then a third through the Byzantine canyons of the Rocks. Finally, he tapped the map with a fingernail. "If I had to guess, I'd say Sadler would expect us to take the straightest route through the Rocks. He'll figure we're in a hurry, and he'll also figure we want to limit our exposure."

"Isn't that what we want?" Sarah asked.

Slocum shook his head. "No. What we want is to get through. An hour one way or another won't matter much, *if* we get through. If we don't, then it won't make any difference what route we take."

"But we only have until tomorrow night to deliver the horses. If we don't get to Fort Stanton by sundown tomorrow, it won't matter what we do. The contract will have been breached."

"I know, Sarah, believe me, I want this to work as much as you do. But we have to be smart."

"Then what should we do?"

"Here, think about this for a minute," he said, placing a fingertip on the map. "This is the beginning of the most direct route. It's the widest canyon, and it goes more than halfway through before we have to choose which way to turn. It bends to the northwest after about a half mile, and a mile deeper into the Rocks, we have to make a decision whether we want to angle this way, to the left, or take the longer, but wider canyon that heads north and slightly east. If I were Ray Sadler, I'd sit right here. . . ." Slocum tapped the union of the main canyon and the two alternates, which formed an irregular y on the map.

"Makes sense. If we come straight in, we have no choice but to pass him there, no matter which way we turn once we get to that point," Rattigan said.

"Right," Slocum agreed. "And I'm betting that's what he's thinking. As near as I could tell from the tracks yesterday, he can't have more than six or seven men with him. For the ambush to work, he's going to have to have most of them right here. He'd probably leave one man at the mouth of the canyon as a spotter. Maybe there'll be one man in another part way down the canyon to relay information. There's three ways in, and if he puts a man on each one, that leaves maybe four at the intersection, cutting his odds way down. And if he covers all three canyons, then he only has a man at each entrance, and one somewhere back in the rocks along each of the routes. Then, he's spread so thin, he can't stop us anyway. What does that tell you?"

Rattigan laughed. "It tells *me* he shoulda brought more men."

Slocum shook his head. "No, it tells you that he's not going to watch all three routes, only the most likely. It's the only way he can do anything to stop us."

"So you're saying we take one of the other routes?" Sarah asked.

"That's exactly what I'm saying."

"But the spotter almost certainly will see us," Rattigan argued.

Slocum nodded. "I know, but if we go through quickly, even if we take the long way, it won't matter. By the time he repositions his men, it'll be too late, especially," and he traced a line with his finger, "if we take this narrow canyon here, then angle this way, cross the main canyon, and pick up the one on the right, right here . . . ," and he tapped the map once more.

"So he thinks we're going along the western route, but we cut across and take the eastern route, but only *after* we get spotted."

"Right. That buys us even more time, because once he starts to move, he's got to follow through. And he's got to move all his men to the same place at the same time, or—"

"Or it's the same as if he'd spread them out in the first place," Sarah finished.

"I like it," Rattigan added. "You're a devious man, John Slocum. And I like that, too. Let's give him hell."

"There's one other thing. . . ."

"And what might that be?"

"I was thinking of going on ahead, scouting things, see what I can see. I'll go right down the middle canyon, so it won't give anything away, and since the horses aren't with me, he'll stay put, thinking maybe we're pulling a fast one."

"Which we are."

"Yes, but not the one he thinks we are."

"What's the point of doing that?" Sarah argued. "You said it yourself, Sadler's going to have most of his men waiting there. Why take the risk? It's foolish."

"Because I might be able to cut the odds a little. If I get in there and raise a little hell, it'll keep them busy."

"You can raise hell with us along, too," Sarah said.

"Not the same way. We'll be hampered by the horses. The herd has to come first. You have to get them moving and keep them moving. If I can get close enough to pin them down, then you'll have a clean shot all the way through. I'll meet you on the other side of Apache Rocks."

"Where?"

Once more, Slocum drew their attention to the map. "Right here, where the Sierra Blanca hits the river. Then it'll be on to Coyote Springs. We'll rest up and run the last leg at first light."

"One thing troubles me, Mister Slocum," Sarah said.

"What's that?"

"Why are you so sure Sadler is going to attack at Apache Rocks? Why wouldn't he wait until Coyote Springs, where it would be easier?"

"Because he'll have another opportunity at Coyote Springs if he makes a mistake here. He'll want to give himself a second chance."

"So we're not out of the woods, even if we make it through Apache Rocks. . . ." It was an observation, not a question, and Sarah seemed subdued, as if she were beginning to despair of ever getting to Fort Stanton.

"No," Slocum said, as kindly as he could, "we're not out of the woods, Sarah. Not until we hand over those horses."

"And even then," Rattigan put it. "We have to get back to Las Cruces with the money. Unless and until you make that mortgage payment, there's a chance Childress can win. All we can do is keep chopping away at the odds. Of course, the best way would be to put a bullet in Tom Childress and stick him in the ground, but that's easier said than done. And it's not the way Jason Bridge wants to win. You know that and I know that. I reckon the only

man in the valley who doesn't know that is Tom
Childress himself. And that's exactly why you don't
want to do it. The last thing you want is to give the
man a chance to say there's no difference between
you, even if it's the last thing he ever says."

Sarah nodded. "I suppose you're right, Mister
Rattigan, and I thank you for saying so."

Rattigan chewed on his lower lip for a moment,
then answered. "Sarah, you have to believe that
there are good people in Las Cruces, people who
will help if they think they have a chance to win.
Nobody wants to stick his neck out if he thinks he's
alone, and that's exactly why Childress has gotten
away with so much for so long. Nobody thinks he'll
get help if he stands up to Childress. Jason's the
first, and it's up to us to see to it that he's not the
last. That's why I'm here. And I think I know a
few others who will pitch in, if we can deliver the
horses and get back to Las Cruces in one piece.
But that's a long skip and jump from where we
are now. You'll just have to hold on, girl. Hold on!
You do that, and we'll do the rest."

Sarah nodded, but there was anything but confidence in the sag of her jaw, and the slackness of
her faint smile.

"We'd better get moving," Slocum said. He walked
to the gray, saddled the big stallion, jammed
the Winchester in its boot, and swung up into
the saddle. "See you at the Tierra Blanca," he
said, tossing off a jaunty salute and flashing
Sarah a grin. Nudging the gray toward her, he
leaned over, cupped her chin in his hand, and
planted a chaste kiss on her lips. "For luck,"
he said.

He spurred the gray out of the canyon and out into the flat country heading north. He looked back once, waved his hat, and turned his attention to the job ahead. At a good clip, it was still almost half an hour to Apache Rocks, and the sooner he got there, the sooner he'd know whether he had guessed right or wrong. And if he had guessed right, the sooner he could begin to improve the odds.

The ride would have been enjoyable, if it hadn't been for what lay ahead. The sun was warm but not hot in the early morning, and a cool breeze out of the north whipped his face. Already, he could see the flattened tops of the buttes, and their brilliant red color seemed to shimmer just above the ground, sometimes appearing almost to vanish as the air began to heat up.

Slocum knew he was giving away a lot. The approach to Apache Rocks was almost dead flat, and the buttes towered high over the valley floor, giving anyone on top a commanding view for miles. But there was no way around them, and there was no choice but to fight their way through.

When he was four miles from the Rocks, he reined in, pulled his field glasses from their case, and trained them on the forbidding heights. He didn't expect to see much, and he had to assume that he had already been spotted. Training the glasses on the extreme left, he traced the rim of the first butte. It was littered with boulders, some solitary and some in clusters, almost any one of which would have been adequate cover for one man.

As he expected, he saw nothing. He scanned the lip of the second huge butte, found the same welter

of broken stone, and again saw no one. There were
two more, and each seemed as deserted as the first
two as he slowly moved the glasses from left to
right, stopping now and then at a likely sentry
position.

The glowering faces of the buttes also offered
niches where a man could hide, but it was unlikely
anyone would have chosen to secret himself any
place but on top. Getting up the wall in a hurry
would be dangerous even without a gun trained
on you, communication would be more difficult and
less covert, and Slocum just gave the walls a cur-
sory glance.

He stuck the glasses back in their leather case,
looped the strap around his neck, and clucked to
the gray. He was wasting time. He kept his eyes
open wide, doing his best to ignore the glare of
sunlight, and hoping something would catch his
eye—some furtive movement, a glint of sunlight
on metal, maybe even a flash from the lenses of
field glasses.

But even getting such a break would change
little. He already believed someone was up there
somewhere. Knowing it reduced the uncertainty a
little, but gave him no advantage at all.

He knew what he had to do, and decided that
he couldn't afford to worry about whether or not
he'd been spotted. He would conduct himself as
he had been, and play with whatever cards Ray
Sadler cared to deal him.

He was less than a mile away when he saw the
flash. Quick, almost illusory, it stabbed at him and
was gone almost before it registered. He wasn't
quite sure where it had come from, but he knew

it was from somewhere toward the central canyon, just to the left. *So*, he thought, *I've guessed right . . . so far.*

Without thinking about it, he reached for the Winchester and removed it, took off the safety, and worked the lever to chamber a round.

Things were about to get a whole lot more interesting. Keeping his eye on the rim, he spurred the gray and galloped toward the mouth of the central canyon.

17

Slocum felt the hair bristle on the back of his neck as he neared the mouth of the canyon. He knew he was being watched, and he knew that somehow word would be passed to Ray Sadler that he was coming. Behind him, the cloud of dust kicked up by the horses told the rest of the story. And that, too, would soon be known to Tom Childress's thugs.

He'd studied the map, and he hoped he knew more about the interlacing canyons through Apache Rocks than Sadler did. Once he passed through the main canyon mouth, he was passing the point of no return. The walls on either side of him rose almost perpendicularly, and he glanced up as he reached the entrance to the main canyon. He had to tilt his head way back to see the rimrock as he passed through.

Once inside, he saw that the canyon opened wider until it was almost five hundred yards across. Looking down its length, he saw a flash of light, then another, and then a third. Not a heliograph, but something—a mirror, perhaps.

He watched the flashes long enough to realize it was not a code, just a signal. He turned in the saddle, but the narrow entrance pinched his field of vision, and he could no longer see the dust cloud. From here on, he would be out of touch with Sarah and Rattigan. All he could do was hope the map was accurate, and that he'd guessed right.

Now, knowing where at least two of Sadler's men were positioned, he had to decide on his next step. The walls were so high that there was no point in trying to engage the Broken C hands in a gun battle to keep them busy—not from the canyon floor. If he got close enough for the Winchester to be effective, he would be under as many as half a dozen guns. If he stayed out of range, he'd be safe, but so would Sadler.

He had to find some way to get up top, and quickly. He remembered several dry washes on the map, some of them looking as if they were blind alleys. But somewhere, he knew, there had to be trails leading to the tops of the buttes. It was how the Apaches managed, and if they could, so could he. Since the horses were taking the left entrance, but only as a feint until they could cross the main canyon and get to the more indirect route through the right side, he wanted to draw Sadler away from them.

He reached the intersection, the place where the herd would cross, and he headed toward it, hoping they could see him. He knew that if he managed to reach the heights, he could occupy the cowhands, and keep them pinned down until he saw the herd cross, then he could make a break for it. It was risky, and time was almost gone, but there was no other choice.

He rode deeper into the narrow defile, the thud of the gray's hooves muffled by layers of sand on the canyon floor. There was the chance that Sadler even now would be moving to head him off, and he searched desperately for some way up to the top.

It took him five minutes to find it, and when he did, he had to fight off the urge to pack it in. There was no way he could manage it on horseback, and he couldn't afford to lead the gray. As near as he could tell, the horse wouldn't be able to make the climb, and he'd have to leave the gray below. The trail disappeared overhead, but seemed to grow progressively narrower as it reached higher. But even if the gray could make it, if they caught him on the way up or down, the horse would be too easy a target, and once the horse was dead, he would be, as well.

Dismounting, he grabbed two ropes, a box of shells for the Winchester, and tugged the big gray in toward the base of the wall. He pulled him into a narrow pocket behind some boulders, and tethered him. Sprinting for the base of the trail, he had the ropes looped over his left shoulder with the Winchester in his right hand.

The first leg of the trail was fairly easygoing, and nearly six feet wide. It slanted uphill at a steep angle, but the footing was secure and he could lean against the pull of gravity and make fairly good time. But when he reached the first turn, everything changed. Doubling back on itself, the trail suddenly narrowed, and it grew steeper. Rock-studded and sandy, it was more suited to moccasins than boots. Twice he nearly slipped and fell, once barely saving himself by grabbing onto the trunk of a twisted scrub oak with roots that were laced like talons into the rock face.

Looking down, he saw that he was only sixty or seventy feet off the floor, and when he looked up, he wondered if he'd miscalculated. The trail seemed to grow narrower and narrower, like railroad tracks receding into the distance. But he pushed on, and turned his back to the wall to try and watch the rim across the canyon. If he'd guessed right, Sadler and his men were somewhere behind him now, and he was looking south, toward Las Cruces.

The herd would be almost to the entrance by now, and he expected at any moment to hear someone shout a warning, but all he heard was the hiss of sand under his feet, and the skitter of dislodged pebbles cascading down to the canyon floor. It was no longer possible for him to see the exchange of mirror signals.

The next fifty feet took him nearly fifteen minutes to climb. It didn't take a mathematician to calculate that he couldn't afford that snail's pace the rest of the way up. He started to move faster, but stopped at a slight bulge in the trail to turn his body around. He could use his hands now, but it meant exposing his back to anyone across the canyon. It wasn't that wide, and he was well within rifle range for the man who'd been watching the approaching herd.

He decided not to worry about things he couldn't control, and concentrated his attention on the precarious footing as he clung like a fly to the sheer rock wall. He'd cut his time in half for the next thirty yards, but he still had nearly fifty feet to go. The trail zigzagged now, almost like switchbacks, and as he clawed his way higher, he was conscious of just how dangerous a route he'd chosen. The trail was little more than a series of shelves; broken ends of stone slabs that long since had fallen to the canyon floor. Some of them were not much wider than the length of his soles, some were even narrower, where his heels would not fit unless he turned his ankle sideways and crab walked with his feet parallel to the wall.

He was sweating now, and the sun was hammering him. His eyes burned from the constant trickle of perspiration, but he needed his hands and his arms to hang on, and there was no chance to wipe the sweat away. His vision kept blurring, and he had to blink away the sting, sometimes stopping for a few seconds until he could see clearly enough to make the next step.

But the trail began to broaden again, sometimes to the generous width of two feet. He looked up, saw that he was only ten feet below the rim, and heaved a sigh. Taking off his hat, he wiped his eyes and forehead with a shirt sleeve, blinked away the last of the sweat, mopped his brow, then wiped his sweaty palms on his pants. He started the last leg with renewed confidence.

He was just below the rim when he heard footsteps. He froze for a second, thinking that someone was on top of the butte, but then he realized the steps were coming from behind him. He turned, almost hanging in space. The footsteps stopped, and suddenly a figure appeared across the canyon.

The man saw him at the same instant. His mouth opened as if to shout something, but he made no sound. Slocum started to swing the Winchester around, but he couldn't move fast enough. The cowboy dropped to the ground and disappeared.

Slocum was a sitting duck. He swung back around and started to scramble up the last few feet. A bullet slammed into the wall, inches from his outstretched hand. Galvanized by the near miss, Slocum grabbed the rim and hauled himself up. One hand lost its grip as a chunk of the rim broke loose, and he scrambled with his feet, trying to find a foothold.

He tossed the Winchester up and over, hanging on with one arm, then grabbed the rock again and tugged himself up. Another shot cracked, and the bullet splattered against the wall so close that splinters of rock pierced his shirt and stung his ribcage.

With all his strength, he dragged himself high enough to get one leg over the rim, twisted, and managed to get his chest and shoulders parallel to the butte. Resting his weight on his ribcage, he grabbed a slab of red stone and pulled himself the rest of the way up over the rim. He scrambled behind the rock, and pressed himself to the ground. Two more quick shots exploded from across the canyon, both bullets ricocheted off the slab, their whines echoing as they faded away.

The Winchester was out in the open, and he couldn't reach it without exposing himself to the man across the narrow canyon. It was long range for a handgun, but there was no alternative. Drawing his Colt, Slocum slithered forward until he could brace the gun against the edge of the rock.

He thumbed back the hammer, looking for the gun-man.

The man was so well hidden, Slocum wasn't quite sure where he was. Under his breath, he mumbled, "Come on, dammit, come on, come on."

Behind him, he knew Sadler had to have heard the gunshots. There was no point in trying to be cautious any longer. The Winchester lay six feet away, so close, but—*what the hell*, he thought.

Rolling clear of the slab of stone, Slocum scrambled for the rifle keeping his eyes on the rim. He tried to hold the Colt steady, but every time he moved, the pistol's muzzle wavered in the air. He could almost reach the Winchester. He stretched out to his full-length, and brushed it with his fingertips, then he grabbed it. That's when the cowboy made his move.

Popping up suddenly ten feet from where Slocum thought he was, he swung his rifle up to his shoulder, but Slocum fired first. The Colt bucked, but he missed. He saw chips of rock fly two feet from the cowboy, who seemed to smile as he aimed the rifle. Slocum thumbed the Colt's hammer again, aimed, and fired once more. The man's rifle went off a split second later, knocked off target by the bullet that slammed into the cowboy's chest, sending him sprawling backward. The rifle pinwheeled, landed on its muzzle, then slid over to the edge, where it teetered for a second, then lay still with its barrel extending out over the rim.

Slocum got to his feet, but couldn't see the cow-boy, and didn't know whether he was dead or just wounded. But there was no time to wait. Slocum dropped the coils of rope and grabbed one end, fashioned a loop, knotted it, and tied it to one of the boulders. He put all his weight onto it and, satisfied that it would hold, tied the second rope to the first, then he tucked the coils out of the way, and sprinted across the butte.

He was going to have to make a quick descent, and there was no way he could risk using the trail. It would mean leaving the ropes behind, but it was a small price to pay. Zigzagging across the butte, he heard yips behind him, and cut toward the rim. A low rumble welled up from the canyon floor, and he knew Rattigan and Sarah were somewhere below him, heading toward the main canyon.

Gunfire exploded up ahead, and he heard men shouting, and the nicker of frightened horses. Racing another thirty yards, he saw puffs of gun smoke, then the backs and shoulders of several men lying on the rim with their rifles aimed down into the canyon.

Another volley crackled, and he dropped to his knees bringing the Winchester to bear, and opened up with three quick shots. The startled men backed away, scrambling to their knees, and looking for the source of the sniper fire.

They were two hundred yards away, and disoriented by his sudden attack.

One of the men spotted him, called to the others, and they swung around, crawling toward the nearest rocks for cover. Slocum was in the open, and dropped to his stomach to crawl closer to the rim. Below him, the steady rumble of the horses echoed out of the canyon. Under fire now, Sadler and his men were unable to concentrate on the herd, and he spotted Sadler himself, shaking a fist and shouting.

Slocum fired two more shots, and Sadler went sprawling. The surprise was effective for now, catching the men off guard and confusing them, but Slocum knew it wouldn't be long before they pulled themselves together—and it wouldn't be long after that that they realized he was alone.

Rolling from one rock to another, Slocum crawled and slithered, getting as close to the rim as he could. Far below, he saw the first of the herd just entering a creek and starting to cross. He leaned out further, and spotted Rattigan and Sarah, their hats in their hands, urging the animals across the creek. They had a quarter-mile run to the far wall, then another two hundred yards to the cut in the rock wall where one of the narrow secondary canyons joined the main one.

Five minutes, Slocum told himself. *If I can hold them for five minutes, we're home free.* Almost as if they'd read his mind, Sadler's men opened fire, and bullets sailed over his head just inches above him. He was pinned down and would have to find a way to hold the cowboys at bay long enough to get clear.

Firing blindly, he emptied the Colt, brought it back and reloaded, then emptied it a second time. It wasn't important to hit anyone as long as the men knew that a mistake might get them killed. Stray bullets were just as deadly as any others.

Pulling the Colt back behind cover, he crawled backward, rolled across an open place, and crept in behind a larger boulder. He could maneuver a little now, and was able to get on his knees to fire without exposing himself too much.

Raising the Winchester, he sighted on the rocks two hundred yards away, waiting for the first mistake.

It wasn't long in coming. One of the hands jumped up and started to race toward him, making a dive for cover, his body arching through the air. Leading his target, Slocum pulled the trigger. He saw blood spurt from the man's shoulder just before he fell to the ground.

Slocum turned his back. It was time to get the hell out of there. He started to run with the reloaded Colt in one hand.

Bullets spanged off the rocks all around him, but he ducked from rock to boulder, zigzagging and feinting as he darted into and out of the open. It was just one hundred yards to the rope now, and he had a long lead. He heard shouts, saw two men pop into the open, and he skidded to a halt. He emptied the Colt once more, and sprinted for the rope and the rim.

18

At the rim, Slocum skidded to a halt, then turned
around and dropped to his stomach. Using the
Winchester, he aimed carefully and fired at the
first target that presented itself. Sadler's men
ducked behind the nearest cover and opened fire,
but Slocum was well protected, and didn't really
care. The rim was right behind him, and all he
wanted was time. The longer he could keep them
pinned, the bigger the head start Rattigan and
Sarah would have with the herd.

Peeking out from behind a rock, he fired again,
then turned his attention to the Colt. He wanted
it loaded when he went down the face of the butte
into the canyon. The rope would get him there
quickly, but there was still a chance that one of
the men would reach the rim before he touched
down, and he wanted the Colt for insurance.

He reloaded the Colt and fired twice more with
the Winchester, then reloaded the rifle, and backed
toward the edge. Grabbing the rope, he tested it
once more to make certain it was securely tied, then

rigged a loose loop around his chest and moved out over the rim. He pushed out, dropped ten or fifteen feet, then braced himself against the wall with his feet, pushed out, and dropped again. It was a giddy sensation watching the rock face slide by.

It would take a minute or two for the men above to realize that he was no longer there, and even then they would be careful in approaching, probably advancing one or two at a time while the others covered. Only when they'd exposed themselves three or four times without drawing fire would they take the chance of charging. By that time, Slocum wanted to be on the canyon floor.

He had gone more than three-quarters of the way before he heard a distant shout. They were coming hard now. Dropping faster, he nearly lost his grip on the rope, and it burned his ribs where it snaked across them. He'd have rope burns that might even draw a little blood, but it was worth it.

He dropped the last ten feet, landed lightly, and twisted out of the rope. Then, realizing that Sadler and his men could come down the same way, he swung the Winchester to his shoulder and aimed at the rope high against the wall, as close to the rim as he could. As he was about to squeeze the trigger, he saw two hat brims, then a pair of faces peering down.

One of the men spotted him and shouted just as he fired. The first shot narrowly missed the rope, and he levered another round into the chamber. The hats and faces had disappeared. Aiming carefully, before the men could think of jerking the rope to throw his aim off, he squeezed the trigger once more, saw the rope part and then come cascading down into the canyon, bouncing off the wall as it collapsed toward him. Three or four feet were left dangling over the rim.

Keeping close to the wall, he sprinted for his horse. It wasn't until he swung into the saddle that it occurred to him that Sadler's men must have left their own mounts somewhere in the canyon. If he could find them and drive them off, he would gain still more time. The most logical place was somewhere down the main canyon near the intersection, and he kicked the gray into a full gallop. Two or three rifle shots broke the silence up above, but the bullets came nowhere close.

Keeping one eye on the ground looking for tell-tale tracks, he raced toward the junction of the y. He was almost there when he spotted the tracks. He reined in, then walked the gray forward, following the welter of hoofprints in the sandy ground. It took him two minutes to find a roomlike gouge in the base of the canyon wall. And there they were—six horses, saddled and ready.

Dismounting, Slocum cut their tethers with his knife, and shook his hat at the horses until they moved reluctantly out of the enclosure. Climbing back onto the gray, he raised the Colt in the air and fired twice. The shots echoed off the walls and sounded like a volley, slapping and cracking back at him from every direction. The horses bolted and broke into the clear. Slocum was right on their heels, yelling and yipping, then he fired once more.

High above, he heard the angry shouts of Sadler and his men as they cursed him and opened fire. But he was too far away for the gunfire to pose a threat. He drove the horses into the eastern arm of the **y** and fired one more shot, enough to keep them running flat-out for quite a while.

It would be hours before Sadler would be able to run them down, and by then, the herd would be well on its way to Coyote Springs.

Slocum sped through the canyon keeping at a full gallop. The horses had begun to scatter now, some forded the shallow creek that ran down the canyon's center, and wandered into one or another of the blind alleys and dry washes that fed into it. Three of the mounts stayed ahead of him running for their lives. Slocum smiled to himself as he saw the canyon's exit suddenly loom ahead as he rounded a sharp turn. Five minutes later, he was out in the open, Apache Rocks falling away behind him like a bad dream.

Far ahead, he could see the dust cloud nearly three miles away, and he knew Rattigan and Sarah had made it through. All he had to do was catch up with them. With any luck, he'd close the gap even before they hit the Sierra Blanca, and they wouldn't even have to slow down.

Slocum drove the gray hard and he didn't bother to look back. It took him an hour to catch the herd, and when he closed on Rattigan, who was riding drag, the big Irishman wheeled his horse and dashed toward him. "We did it, John, we did it! Oh, boy, I never thought we'd pull it off, but, by God, we did it!"

"We're not home free yet, Phil," Slocum warned.

Sarah saw him then and spurred her sorrel over. Leaning over to kiss him, she almost fell from the saddle. Her face was wreathed in smiles. "Thank

God, you're all right," she said. "We heard the gun-fire, and I got terribly frightened. Phil wanted to go back, but I wouldn't let him. I told him you would want him to stay with the herd. It was hard to convince him, but I finally managed."

Rattigan chuckled. "It was that rifle of hers that convinced me," he said. "She actually threatened to shoot me, can you believe it? Said all I would manage to do is foul things up. You were counting on us pushing through and running for it. She said I could have gotten us both killed."

Slocum smiled. "I don't know if it would have come to that, but I'm glad you listened to her."

"So, how many of them are left?" Rattigan asked.

"I'm not sure. I know I hit three of them, but I have no idea how badly. The main thing was to keep them pinned down until you got through. I ran their horses off and it'll be hours before they can come after us. But they will come after us, make no mistake about that."

"The springs, do you think, John?"

Slocum nodded. "Yeah, I do. We'll be safe here, but once we head out in the morning, I'd look for trouble."

"It's a straight shot to Fort Stanton from there. We should be able to make it all right, don't you think?"

"I hope so, Phil. Let's push on. I want to get to Coyote Springs by nightfall. We get caught in the open, there'll be hell to pay."

The trip took five hours. By five o'clock in the afternoon, Slocum was looking over his shoulder. More than likely, he thought, Sadler's got his horses back by now. And he'll be riding hell for leather.

When the last canyon, Coyote Springs nestled at its center, came into view, the sun was already beginning to slip toward the peaks of the Black Mountains. There was less than an hour of good light left, and Slocum urged his companions to hurry.

They entered the canyon and pushed the horses to the springs, where they waded out into the water and drank their fill. There was plenty of grass, and the horses lost no time in sampling it. Unlike the night before, there was no place they could pen the herd, and they would have to hope that Sadler didn't make a move before daylight.

Once more, they were faced with the prospect of little sleep and less rest, but there was no other way to do it. Slocum took the first watch again.

When Rattigan and Sarah turned in, Slocum resaddled their mounts, and the gray. If Sadler struck during the night, there would be no time to tend to their mounts.

It was one o'clock in the morning when Sarah strode toward him out of the dark. She carried her rifle, but she was barefoot, and her shirt was already unbuttoned. Planting herself in front of him, she smiled. In the moonlight, she looked almost ghostly. There were dark hollows under her eyes, and pockets of shadow at her throat. She stripped off her shirt, gave him a crooked grin, and asked, "Are you ready, Mister Slocum?"

Unbuttoning her jeans, she jerked them down around her knees and kicked them aside. For a brief instant, he thought about sending her back to bed, but as she stepped closer to him, he knew there was no way he could do it.

Getting to his feet, he started to unbutton his shirt. Sarah knelt in front of him and unbuckled his belt, then undid his fly and jerked his jeans down to his ankles. Looking up at him, she pushed his erection to one side and said, "I see you *are* ready. The only question in my mind is whether it's again or still?"

"Does it matter?"

"No, sir, it doesn't." She stood up and stretched her arms over her head, then turned sideways for a moment, grinning at him over her shoulder. "Am I too tall, do you think?"

"No, Ma'am, you're not too tall. You're just about perfect."

He kicked off his boots then, with Sarah's help. When his feet were free, she grabbed him by the cock and tugged him deeper into the brush. "My mother always used to say women led my father around by his private parts. Now I see what she meant."

This time, it was his turn to kneel. He slid his hands along the backs of her thighs, and up over her ribs, then he brought them forward to cup her breasts for a moment. He rested a cheek against her thick bush and inhaled her musky scent for a moment, then slid his hands down over her stomach, and teased the curls with his fingers. Then, he spread her thighs and leaned forward to slide his tongue into the dark tangle.

She shivered, and he backed away for a moment. In the moonlight, little pearls glittered in the tight curls, and he caught one on the tip of his tongue, then sat down as her hands pressed against his shoulders.

The sand was gritty beneath him, but he ignored the discomfort as Sarah straddled him. Reaching up to her, he took her hands as she lowered herself toward him. Freeing her right hand, she grabbed his cock, steadied it, and buried its head between her fleshy lips, and lowered herself all the way down, trembling as a moan escaped her. She threw her head back, and moaned again as he rocked his hips once, then again.

Bracing herself on his chest, she lifted herself up. He felt the cool breeze on the slickness she left behind, and groaned when she swallowed him again, this time grinding against his hips. Up again, then down, she was moving slowly, deliberately, her tongue darting between her lips with every descent, vanishing every time she rose.

He caught her by the hips then, and started to settle into a rhythm. She matched it, then increased the pace a little, then a little more. She leaned forward to kiss him, and he felt the heaviness of her breasts swaying against him, the prod of her nipples teasing him with every pass.

Faster now, and faster still, first one, then the other increasing the tempo. She was moaning louder now, paying no attention to anything but the insistent probe of him, and the rocking of her hips.

Her cries grew more intense, almost as if she were losing control, and he asked if he were hurting her.

She shook her head violently, lashing him with her long hair, "No, no, no," she moaned. "No, no, you're not hurting me." The words exploded in gasps, then Sarah threw her head back and trembled as she strained to go faster and faster. She was pounding against him now, and he matched her thrust for thrust.

His hands on her hips, he brought her down, slowing the pace, probing less often but more deeply, and twisting from side to side. He felt the trickle of her juices down over his thighs, and smelled the musky scent of her. As she insisted they go faster once more, he gave in, letting her set the pace, closing his eyes and shutting off everything but the indescribable sensation of her muscles rippling along the length of him—teasing, squeezing, until he thought she meant to swallow him entirely.

She exploded then, crying out in one long shuddering moan, and fell forward heavily, wrapping her arms around his neck. Her breath was hot on his cheek, and when she whispered, it was almost a sob, "God, I love you, John Slocum," she said. "Lord knows, I don't want to, but I do."

He stroked her then, feeling her heart pounding against his ribs as his fingers traced the curves of her ass, and counted the bones of her spine. She snuggled her hips closer.

"Stay this way just another minute, please," she asked.

"As long as you want," he whispered.

And the night closed in around him again. He lay there, watching the moon, its highlights on her muscled back, and the swell of her ass, until she started to breathe deeply, and he knew she had fallen asleep.

He knew that Ray Sadler was out there somewhere in the dark. But for the moment, it couldn't have mattered less.

19

Slocum stayed up all night. Well before the first hint of gray brightened the sky, and while the moon was still filling the canyon with silver and shadow, he woke Sarah, half expecting that she would be angry with him. He felt a little foolish, as if he had somehow betrayed her, and in doing so, somehow tainted what he was trying to do for her and Jason. But if she felt the same, there was no hint of it in the smile she gave him.

"I guess I'd better go wake Mister Rattigan," she said.

Slocum nodded in agreement. "I'd get dressed first, though. You don't want Phil thinking he's died and gone to heaven."

"Do I look that bad?"

"On the contrary."

She noticed that he seemed subdued. "Is there anything wrong?" she asked.

"I'm sorry about last night," he said.

"Whatever for? I'm a big girl, John. If you think you took advantage of me, think again. It was me who came to you, remember?"

"That's something I don't think I'll ever forget."

He smiled, but it was distant, even sad, and she nodded. "Look," she said, "if you think I'm going to try to change you, to make you stay here, don't worry about it. If you want to stay, you'll stay. If not, you won't. I know that. Knew it before I ever came to you. I know what I said last night, and I meant it. But that doesn't change anything. I don't want you to do anything you don't want to do. All right?"

"All right."

"We'll talk about it later, if you want. If not, I'll never mention it again." She started pulling on her clothes, buttoned her shirt, and picked up her rifle. She started to walk toward the campsite, stopped, and looked back over her shoulder. "Thank you," she said.

Slocum followed her a few minutes later. Rattigan wasn't easy to rouse, and Slocum realized that the rugged trip was taking a toll on him. "We're almost there, Phil," he said.

"I can tell that by my aching bones. I have a dozen joints I never knew about, and rheumatism in every blessed one." He laughed, then stretched to try to loosen up. Pulling on his boots, he asked, "So, you think Sadler's waiting for us up ahead, do you?"

"Yup. I wish we could circle the canyon, but we'll lose too much time."

"Maybe we should do the same thing we did last time. The herd's been fed and watered, maybe we should just run like hell out the other end and leave it to him to stop us if he can."

"I don't think we have any choice."

"I'm surprised he didn't hit us during the night. It ain't like him to take the long way around. Maybe he ain't even here. Maybe you done better than you knew, running off his horses. Maybe. . . ."

"Maybe there's a pot of gold at the end of every rainbow."

"You mean there isn't? But me old mither said. . . ."

"You're too Irish by half, Mister Rattigan," Sarah joked.

"You can't never be too rich or too Irish, Miss Bridge," he said. "Course, I can speak from experience about only one of the two. I'll leave it to you to figure out which."

"I think we'd better forget about breakfast," Slocum interrupted. It'd be best if we got moving before sunup. We can take it slow, but we just might manage to surprise Mister Sadler, and even if we don't, it'll make his job that much harder."

"I'm all for that," Rattigan said. "Let's get moving."

Breaking camp was easy with no fire to worry about and no meal to make. The horses were all saddled and ready, and Slocum was the first to mount up. He moved toward the springs and waited for the others to join him. The herd seemed nervous, and he wondered if Sadler was closer than he thought, or if it was the movement in the half-darkness that made the animals skittish.

The moon was going down, and Slocum wanted the herd in a tight bunch before they lost the advantage of its light. If they timed it right, they would be at the canyon exit as the moon went down and would have the darkness to cover them. As soon as Rattigan joined him, the two men started gathering the herd together. Sarah pitched in when she arrived, and soon all the horses were together. The moon was already slipping below the horizon, and the shadows deepened as the drovers started to move west.

Ahead, through the last of the moonlight, Slocum could just make out the exit from the canyon, and he started to yip, getting the horses moving faster. Rattigan pulled his gun, but Slocum shouted not to use it. "Save your ammunition," he said.

The herd was picking up speed as the open space beyond the canyon rushed toward it. Faster and faster they went, until the horses were at a full gallop. The exit was narrow, and the herd seemed instinctively to flatten itself into a narrow band of glistening horseflesh to accommodate the squeeze without slowing down.

When the first horses burst through into the open plains, it seemed almost like a signal, and the moon suddenly vanished, leaving dark shadow where the pewter glaze had been. Riding at a breakneck pace, Slocum followed the animals out into the clear, and he strained to see the lead horses. He could just pick out Rattigan and Sarah now, phantoms on horseback, and it was only the difference in their sizes that told him who was who.

And the first pistol shot cracked an instant later. He leaned toward the figure he thought to be Rattigan, but there was no telltale wisp of gun smoke that would look gray against the blackness. The shot had come from elsewhere. Only when the second shot exploded was he able to locate its source.

He turned toward the sound to see four figures racing toward him through the night. He shouted to Rattigan, "Phil, you and Sarah are on your own," then he turned the gray and charged toward the attacking horsemen.

More gunfire exploded, and Slocum could see the deadly tongues of flame licking at him, with plumes of gray smoke swirling in the brief instant of illumination. Behind the muzzle flashes, he could see swatches of color as the gunmen were bathed momentarily in light.

Bullets whined overhead as the gunmen tried to steady their aims, but the galloping horses made accuracy all but impossible at two hundred yards.

Slocum skidded to a halt and dismounted, jerking the Winchester from its boot and patting his pocket to make sure he had ammunition for it.

He knelt beside a clump of mesquite, straining through the darkness to spot the charging riders. The bulky shadows were faintly etched against the blackness behind them, and he waited for another shot to home in on them. When it came, he was ready. He lead the tongue of flame by a couple of feet, and squeezed the trigger. He heard a groan, then a thud as something heavy hit the ground. There was a scraping sound, and then someone shouted. He realized that his target had fallen from the saddle, and was being dragged across the rocky sand with one foot caught in a stirrup.

The charging horsemen slowed, and Slocum leaned toward them, trying to spot another target. Another thud was followed by a scream and then a moan. The dragged man must have slammed into something, maybe a cactus, maybe a boulder, but the scraping sound of the dragging stopped, and so did the hoofbeats.

"Slocum . . . ?"

He recognized Ray Sadler's voice echoing through the night as if issuing from the mouth of a well. "Slocum . . . ? You're a dead man, Slocum. You know that?"

A furious volley exploded, but the bullets came nowhere close. Sadler was firing blindly, trying to frighten him, and force him to make a move and give away his location.

"Slocum, you hear me?"

Resisting the temptation to respond, Slocum lay on the sand. Far behind him, the sound of the galloping herd was fading away. He knew he could stay there and keep Sadler busy while Rattigan and Sarah pushed on toward Fort Stanton. With the night to cover him, he could hold Sadler for a couple of hours. He had done it once, and it had worked. But this time, he wasn't going to settle for something so tame. Ray Sadler wanted him? All right, he wanted Sadler just as badly. And before the sun came up, he would have him, dead or alive.

Slocum listened in the darkness for a footstep, the hiss of a careless boot heel on the sand, or the cocking of a gun. But it was deathly silent. It seemed almost as if Sadler and his men had vanished into thin air. Not even the dull thud of a hoof on the ground broke the stillness.

Slocum got to his knees, then backed away from the mesquite. He knew Sadler had seen the spurt of flame from his last shot, and he wanted to put some distance between him and the point where Sadler's attention was fixed.

He'd gone fifteen feet when three guns opened up all at once. He heard the bullets snicking through the mesquite, the snapping of stiff twigs, and the sudden brittle rain of leaves scattering through branches.

Once more, Sadler called to him. "Slocum, how'd you like that? Did we come close, cowboy? We'll be closer next time."

Slocum moved another few feet, then stopped to reorient himself. He'd seen where the shots had come from, and realized that Sadler's men were bunched together. Instead of spreading out to surround him if they could, they were clinging to one another, afraid of shooting each other by accident. It was sensible, but it made them an easy target.

Still holding his fire, he moved another ten feet, angling away from them, and hoping to circle around behind and take them by surprise. If he could get behind them, he could risk a shot without having the muzzle flash give away his location. Sound was less useful in the darkness. It seemed to come from every place at once and no place at all.

He heard a horse then; a nicker, thumping, nervous hooves, but it came from a distance, and he was unable to distinguish the animal in the darkness.

"Slocum," Sadler taunted, "you know what's going to happen to that woman, don't you? When I catch her—and I *will* catch her—I'm gonna climb in the saddle, Slocum, and ride her till she's played out." He laughed then, a brittle sound tinged with rage, but Slocum refused to take the bait.

He had nothing but time, and when the time was right, he would make his move. But not before.

Someone ran then, with heavy steps that charged ahead, but the runner tripped and sprawled, and cursed as he scrambled back to his feet. Slocum took advantage of the distraction to move another twenty feet. Moving cautiously on tiptoe, he started to circle back now, cutting toward the sound of Sadler's voice.

Another volley erupted, and he could see that he was almost in line with the three men. But in the bottled lightning of the muzzle flashes, he couldn't tell whether they were advancing or standing pat, and he moved another five yards, turning now to watch. He glanced at the sky for a moment and saw that is was just the least bit gray. Some of the stars had vanished, and he guessed he had another twenty minutes of total darkness. Then the sky would begin to brighten.

He wasn't worried, but wanted to reduce the odds a little before first light. He reached down and groped on the sand for a rock. Finding one the size of his fist, he closed his fingers around it, hefted it, and tossed it as far as he could back the way he'd come.

It landed with a crack against another rock, and once more the night exploded into gunfire. But this time, Slocum didn't let the opportunity pass. As the muzzles flashed, he aimed at the center figure, fired quickly three times, then hit the deck.

His second shot had found its target, and the third had also hit someone, probably the same man.

"Callahan?" the voice was Sadler's, but this time a hoarse whisper. "Callahan? You hit?"

A groan was the only response. "Christ!" Sadler was getting frustrated, and that was perfect. The madder he got, the more reckless he'd be. He was playing right into Slocum's hands.

"That was stupid, Slocum. We know where you are now."

Once more, Slocum ignored the taunt, and crawled as fast as he could on his stomach, bumping once into a cholla, and snapping off a few of its spines in the meat of his forearm. He lay there for a moment, rolling up his sleeve and feeling for the stiff little needles. He plucked them out one at a time, then ran his fingertips over his forearm to make sure he'd gotten them all. His forearm stung, and was damp and sticky where blood oozed from the dozen or so punctures.

The sky had brightened a little more, and he could see them now, just dim shapes against the dark gray. He couldn't tell which one was Sadler, but it didn't matter. He lay there watching, waiting. Just a little longer, he thought, a little longer. He was on his stomach, and he had the rifle ready now, the Colt was back in its holster, empty. He didn't want to risk the noise of reloading.

He sighted on the nearer of the two shapes. They were both thirty yards away and heading toward him. Because they were standing, they didn't seem to realize they stood out in relief while Slocum's prostrate form was still indistinguishable from the ground. And he squeezed the trigger. The bullet slammed into the target chest high, sent the shadow sprawling, and the second figure dove to the ground.

Once more, that brittle laugh. "You and me, now, Slocum," Sadler yelled.

Sadler emptied his pistol in rage, and Slocum got to his feet then, charging toward him. He could just make out Sadler's shape as he scrambled to his left, the movement giving him away. Slocum closed on him, launching himself through the air as Sadler groped in the near darkness for another gun.

He swung the Winchester like a club, heard the crack of walnut on bone, then yanked Sadler to his feet. But the cowboy had found what he was looking for. He had a pistol in his hand and was bringing it up as Slocum turned the Winchester quickly and fired, point blank. The impact of the bullet shattered bone and Sadler fell over backward. The gun in his hand went off, the bullet sailing wildly off into the breaking dawn.

Then he lay still.

20

Jason Bridge looked at the stack of bills on the table. His face wore a stunned expression. "I can't believe it," he said. "You did it. I just can't believe it."

"Count it again," Rattigan suggested, laughing. "Or I will, if you don't mind a short count."

"Ten thousand dollars. That solves our problem, and then some." Jason looked at Slocum. "I don't know how to thank you," he said.

"You're not out of the woods yet, Jason. There's still the matter of making the payment."

"I know, but. . . ."

"Ray Sadler is dead," Sarah said. "What can stop us now? It's too late to stop us."

"Sure, Sadler's dead. And Tom Childress doesn't know it. Not yet, anyway," Rattigan said. "It's smooth sailing from here on in."

"I wish I could be sure of that," Slocum argued. "You said that Childress has the bank in his hip pocket. And the banker, too."

Jason nodded. "Right. Tyler Hutchins is just

a puppet. Childress pulls the strings, and Tyler dances. But if I show up with the money a few days early, what can he possibly do? He'll have to take the payment. He'll do it, I'm certain of that. There's no reason not to."

"No reason, maybe, except Tom Childress," Slocum said. "If he's as afraid of Childress as you said, Hutchins will try to find a reason not to take the money. And there's still Walter Kennedy to deal with. The sheriff can try to impound the money, just like he did the horses. All he has to do is stick it in his desk drawer until the deadline passes."

"I should have killed him when I had the chance," Jason said. "It would have been so easy."

Sarah shook her head. "No, Jason, that's not the way to do it. You know that and so do I. No, we'll just have to find some other way."

"I'll handle it," Rattigan said, getting to his feet. He groaned, rubbed his aching knees, and started for the door in a hurry.

"Where are you going, Phil?" Jason asked. "What's the big rush?"

"I want to talk to a few people, is all. Nothing serious. Nothing dangerous. Just a little small town business." He smiled mysteriously and disappeared through the door, letting the screen bang closed behind him.

"Phil," Slocum called, getting to his feet, "you want me to come with you?"

A disembodied voice shouted back, "Not necessary, Johnny. It's about time folks like me started leaning on each other, instead of some stranger with a funny accent. Southern, I believe it is."

Slocum laughed, shook his head helplessly, and sat back down.

"Now I'm worried," Sarah said. "Suppose something happens? Suppose Slocum's right? Suppose. . . ."

"You can suppose all you please, Sarah, but I don't give a damn what happens. I am going to make that payment first thing in the morning, and nobody, not Walter Kennedy, not Tyler Hutchins, not even Tom Childress, is going to stop me."

He looked at Slocum and then at Sarah. "You make a good team," he said.

Sarah smiled, glanced at Slocum, then answered, "Not for long. I have a funny feeling Mister Slocum will be moving on soon."

Jason looked at Sarah, puzzled by something in her voice, then at Slocum. "That right?" he asked. "You moving on?"

Slocum nodded. "Yup. Soon as you make the mortgage payment."

Jason looked thoughtful, then picked up the stack of bills in front of him, counted several off the top, neatened them, and handed them to Slocum.

"That's three hundred dollars, Jason, three months pay—or thereabouts. I can't take it."

"Sure you can. You did a month's work every day for six days. Fair's fair."

"Jason, I—"

Bridge held up a hand to silence him. "No argument, Mister Slocum. If it weren't for you, everything we have would be gone. It's the least I can do."

Reluctantly, Slocum took the bills, folded them, and tucked them into his pocket. "I think I'm going to get some sleep," he said. "It's been a rough few days. And tomorrow won't be any easier, I've a feeling."

"I'll stay up," Jason said. "Somebody ought to keep an eye out and a hammer cocked, just in case."

Slocum moved toward the door. "Good night."

"See you in the morning," Jason said. "Bright and early."

"Good night, Mister Slocum," Sarah added, her voice quavering.

She stared at him over her brother's shoulder, her face threatening to shatter into a hundred pieces. Slocum went out the door.

Once in the barn, he curled his gun belt beside his makeshift bed, sat down, and pulled off his boots. He lay back, pulled the blanket over him, and closed his eyes. But he knew he wouldn't sleep. He wondered whether Sarah would come to see him. He wondered, too, whether he wanted her to. He couldn't possibly stay on in Las Cruces. It wasn't him, it wasn't the kind of life he was meant to live. It was a painful truth to confront, but there it was.

An hour went by, the barn was filled with darkness; with silence, his breathing, and a thousand questions—questions about who he was, where he was going, and how his life would end.

He thought about settling down more often than he cared to, sometimes even about having a family, bouncing a baby on his knee, watching a son learn to shoot, and catching trout in a brook high in the mountains together.

He wondered what it would be like to have a

little girl. Would she have the same long legs as
Sarah? Would she have the same wanderlust as
her father? But they were pointless questions, really, because there was no way it would ever happen,
no matter how much he might want it to. And
the truth was, he wanted it more than he dared
admit.

When he heard footsteps approaching the barn,
he knew he was going to have to confront all those
questions once more. He saw a figure in the doorway outlined against the night.

"Are you sleeping, John?" Sarah whispered. For
a moment, he considered pretending that he was,
but that was the coward's way.

"No," he said. He watched as she came toward him
tentatively, her steps slow and uncertain. When she
reached his makeshift bed, she leaned forward, and
he reached out to take her hand.

Her fingers squeezed his, and she sat beside him.
"I just want to stay here tonight, with you," she
said. "No sex, just companionship, if that's what
you want."

"All right," he whispered. He wrapped her in his
arms and swirled the blanket around her. She lay
beside him, and he could feel her heart beating
against his chest. For a long time, she didn't say
anything. Then, with her lips close to his ear, she
whispered, "It would have been wonderful."

"Yes," he answered.

She drifted off to sleep, but he lay there awake,
watching the night sky through the barn door—
the pageant of the stars, the sudden wash of moonlight, then its steady fade to black again.

And when the sun came up, she was still there,

fast asleep. Jason Bridge appeared in the doorway, tiptoed toward him, and held a finger to his lips before beckoning Slocum outside. Extricating himself carefully, Slocum got up and followed Jason out into the sunlight.

"I hope you let her down easy," he said. "She's a good woman. The best. I want her to be happy."

Slocum nodded. "Yes, me too."

"You're welcome to stay on, Slocum. You know that. No pressure. Sarah knows her own mind, but she respects what other people think, what they want to do, how they want to lead their own lives."

"I know that, Jason, but it would be too hard for me. I don't think I could handle it."

Jason nodded. "Fair enough."

They heard hoofbeats then, and Jason looked frightened. He ran to the house and came back with his shotgun. "You'd better wake Sarah," he said.

Slocum went into the barn, shook Sarah by the shoulder, and said, "Someone's coming."

He strapped on his gun belt. Grabbing his rifle, he went back outside as a solitary rider appeared on the road. Behind him, a cloud of dust hung in the air, more than what could have been kicked up by a single horse.

The rider approached at a gallop, and Slocum recognized the substantial figure of Rattigan. "It's Phil!" he shouted, then ran down the lane and toward the road. Jason, still weak from his wounds, lagged behind.

"Phil," Slocum hollered, "what's going on? What are you doing here?"

Turning to look over his shoulder, Rattigan said, "I brought some company along."

"Company—what sort of company?" Jason asked.

Rattigan smiled. "Let's just say a few concerned citizens. I figured maybe it was about time we let Mister Tyler Hutchins know that it's *our* bank as much as it's his, and that Tom Childress has nothing to say about it."

"What are you talking about?"

Rattigan shrugged. "It's people, Jason, just plain folks. The folks who live here in the valley, and who are as sick and tired of Tom Childress as you are. They've had enough, and they're going to back you. Tyler Hutchins is going to take that payment if I have to force feed him the bills one at a time. If Walter Kennedy wants to do something about it, he's welcome to try, but somehow I don't think that will happen. Walter is finished, and he knows it. So's Tom Childress. He may not know it yet, but he will, Jason, he will."

"But—"

Rattigan shook a finger at him. "Jason, Jason, don't you see? Childress did what he did because we stood around with our thumbs in our galluses watching him do it. But no more. We're taking back Las Cruces, taking back our lives. We're going to walk on two legs like men are meant to, and it's about damned time."

"I don't know what to say. . . ."

"Don't say nothing. Just get in the saddle and come on, man. You've got a mortgage to pay." He grinned, and winked at Slocum. "Hurry up now, time's awastin'."

Jason raced back toward the house, shouting to

Sarah, but his words were so hasty they tumbled unintelligibly from his mouth.

Rattigan looked at Slocum. "You know, Johnny, you had more than a little to do with this, don't you?"

Slocum shrugged.

"Now, don't be goin' all modest on us. You made us think about what we were doing, how we'd let things slip away. Once we decided to stand back and do nothing, it got to be a habit. And habits are hard to break. But you did it. You stood up to Sadler. You showed us how."

"I think you're giving me too much credit."

Rattigan shook his head. "No, no, not at all. We gave Childress too much credit, and we didn't give ourselves enough. But that's all over now. We're back in the saddle, and we'll decide which way to ride. Thanks to you." He waved frantically to someone near the house.

Slocum turned to see Jason and Sarah riding toward him. When they came abreast of Rattigan, Jason said, "Aren't you coming, Mister Slocum? I would think you'd want to be there for the finish. . . ."

Slocum smiled. "I think I already am."

Sarah nudged her horse close to him, leaned over, and closed her eyes. He leaned forward, kissed her lightly on the lips, and backed away. She opened her eyes slowly. "That was the last one, wasn't it?"

He nodded.

"Will you be here when we get back?"

He shook his head.

"Goodbye, then."

He watched them as they rode toward town.

Kennedy and the others in the barn would have to be dealt with at some point, Slocum knew. But they could wait, he decided. Not until they were out of sight did he turn toward the barn. He felt empty inside.

But he was used to it.